The Leprechaun's Curse

by

Jane Greenhill

Cover Art by *Lea Schizas*

The Wild Rose Press, Inc.
PO Box 708
Adams Basin, NY 14410-0708
Visit us at www.thewildrosepress.com

Publishing History
First Edition, 2024
Trade Paperback ISBN 978-1-5092-5630-3
Digital ISBN 978-1-5092-5631-0

Published in the United States of America

Dedication

To Geoff, Adam, and Liam—for the encouragement and
beta reading.
Mary Sue—my personal cheerleader
Teresa—my Kentucky BFF and mentor
Lea—thank you for your enthusiasm for Elmville's story
Lady Caroline—you continue to amaze me!!
To my readers—may the leprechauns dance over your
bed and bring you sweet dreams.

Chapter 1

Did you know there is over a gallon of blood in the human body? Elmville actually went to a library and checked in an Encyclopedia the first time he killed someone. (Encyclopedias for those who are too young to know it was the first method of searching, where you actually had to get off your butt and go to a library instead of sitting on your comfy couch and typing.)Well, not at the time did he venture out. I mean, he had some other things on his plate, so to speak, but immediately afterward when his adrenaline came back down to normal and he was drinking his after-kill drink of peppermint tea with a touch of honey. Yumm. Though he did favor cotton candy and candied apples, which just depended on the time of year and the degree of celebration.

I have to say he didn't kill needlessly, and he did save a dog. Not everyone deserves killing, but in this instance…. Not to say he acted as a judge and jury or executioner, but let me tell you his story and I'm sure you'll agree. So, put the kettle on, get out your tea, and if you want a biscuit, 'cause chocolate biscuits always go well with a spot of tea. Put your feet up on that comfy ottoman, not forgetting the blanket your great-grandmother crocheted for you, and let's get the show on the road, so to speak.

I'll start at the very beginning—a very good spot to

start. Now I've given you an earworm, we'll commence.

Chapter 2

DRURIE: NOW

I climbed through the knot in the tree and slid down into the funnel of the tree trunk. While it was a reminiscence of being a kid on the playground, the reason I was there meeting with King Cloverdale wasn't fun. In fact, I was going to get reamed out royally.

"He's waiting for you." The owl screeched, his head on a swivel, watching and seeking all. "Take your hat off. You should know better."

"Sorry, I forgot." I was wearing my number two's, my fancy vest and breeches in royal blue, accented with gold buttons.

"Drurie, how nice of you to join me. I hope it wasn't too much of an inconvenience." King Cloverdale's voice reaped in sarcasm.

I wasn't sure if I should answer or just nod, so I did both. "Sorry, sir. It won't happen again."

"Never mind, we haven't got time to go into all your iniquities. Tell me about your brother. Have you solved the issues we constantly encounter with Elmville?"

"Sir, the crux is, and I don't mean to be a brathadoir, a snitch."

"Son, I know what a brathadoir is. You don't need

to explain it to me." His sigh rustled the leaves lining the tunnel.

"Right, sorry, sir. Elmville lost his leprechaun coin to the Tobin family. He's inflicted havoc over the centuries to try and get it back."

King Cloverdale rubbed his beard, pulling the coarse white hairs into a triangle. "Umm, so you're saying the coin, which helps to balance the good and evil of a leprechaun, is out of whack. That's why I have insomnia because he lost his stupid coin?"

"Yes, sir, in a nutshell." Relief filled my body, and the weight of the world was removed from my shoulders. I knew the King was upset but a burden shared and all. I don't know how Atlas managed it, but then his brothers probably didn't lose their coins.

"So, doesn't it make sense you need to get it back?" King Cloverdale nodded, as did every being in the room. Bunch of Cloverdale kissers. "Remember, though, it has to be returned to where it was lost."

"Yes, he's got a real hate on for the Tobin family."

Chapter 3

KITTY
LAS VEGAS, U.S.A.
3 MONTHS AGO

I shifted gears in mom's 2014 Honda Civic, my head bobbing as I sang along to the radio cranked to Luke Bryan's "Knockin'Boots." Nevada's State Road Route 375 was the most destitute highway I had ever traveled. No traffic lights, no streetlights, no nothing. The only company was Luke and the scrub brushes lining the highway, and the occasional cacti breaking up the monotony.

Clouds played peek-a-boo with a full moon. Headlights from a transport truck appeared like two beacons, reminding me I wasn't alone on the road. The enormous vehicle sped past, shaking the car as I fought for control. I lowered the window, the sound of a coyote howling in the distance, surprisingly in tune with Luke.

Static replaced Luke's voice as clouds covered the moon. The only light remaining was from the high beams. Stabbing at the radio buttons, the static rose into a high-pitched screech, and I instinctively covered my ears with my hands.

My phone buzzed as Mom's name flashed. I glanced up to see my headlights illuminating a short green man standing in the middle of the road. Warts covered his prominently hooked nose, his face creased with inch-deep wrinkles. A green bowler hat with a silver buckle on the front was resting on ears larger than pancakes. A happenstance grin revealed razor-sharp teeth and clapping revealed fingernails talon-sharp. He barely came to the bumper of my car, his short legs dressed in tartan shorts, and his feet jammed into slippers with the toes curled. Little silver bells were attached to the top. I slammed on the brakes, yet the speed didn't lessen. Slapping my sweaty hands back onto the steering wheel, I attempted to regain control of the car. The wheel spun like a Ferris wheel, as I endeavored to avoid the creature.

The car roared off the asphalt, crushing the scrub brush, the undercarriage of the car scraping against rock from the Pahranagat Range as the vehicle picked up speed, careening across the open landscape, plowing into the base of a billboard advertising a local brothel, the driver's side crimping like an accordion. My head hit the steering wheel, the pillow of an airbag deploying as the car came to a stop.

"Are you okay?" a male voice demanded, as I struggled to get out. "Stay where you are. Cell reception is crap out here, but lucky for you I do know some first aid."

Cringing, I was relieved to see he was the full height and size of a real man. A slight beard covered his face and a small gold earring accented one normal-sized ear. My rescuer wore a Las Vegas Knights baseball cap and a Raiders t-shirt—nothing tartan there.

The man lifted me out of the car, supporting my head and back, and laid me gently on the ground, avoiding the cactus and spiky brush.

"Your head looks okay, though it wouldn't hurt to have a CT scan, cause you never know what's going on inside your noggin. You might have whiplash or even a concussion." Lights from his truck lit up the area and I flinched when I saw the damage to Mom's car.

"My mom's going to kill me." My sobs filled the night air, Luke's song on repeat.

"I'm sure once she knows you're okay, she'll be fine. I'll call her once we get you to the hospital." Like I was made of glass, he lifted me and carried me to the truck.

"I'm Fred Tobin. What's your name?" he asked as I sat on the passenger side of his F150 pickup.

"Kitty."

Elvis Presley singing "Viva Las Vegas" interrupted the night as I fished the phone out of my jacket pocket. Ben's name flashed up on the screen with the screen saver of the two of us at table 53 at the top of the Eiffel Tower.

"Ben, can I call you back?" My head was woozy from the collision with the cacti. "I've had a bit of an accident."

"Sure, one question—do you and your mom have current passports?" Ben asked, his thick Boston accent yelling into the phone. When Ben called, my phone automatically went into speaker mode without having to push any buttons.

"Yes, we just got them renewed." Ben tended to snowplow over anything that didn't concern him. Case in point. I'd discovered early you couldn't overwhelm him with too many issues at once and it appeared he had his plate full with his boss' and his problems. "Ben,

I'm at the junction of—"

"Okay, pack your bags because you're heading to Ireland. Wicked Pissah!" Ben hung up before I could say another word.

"Was that your boyfriend?" Fred asked, bugs flying into the light of his beams. "He sure is loud."

"No, definitely not a boyfriend," I said, then internally slapped myself. This guy, while he did rescue me, could be a serial killer for all I know. He could be planning to dump my body. Though I was reassured by the picture of a smiling blonde and two little girls tucked into his rear-view mirror. I did have the find a phone app. My mother liked to keep an eye on me. So good thing if indeed I was in the hands of a serial killer.

"What caused you to careen off the road? I don't smell any alcohol, and you're too upset to be high."

"A little green man." I bit my lip as even to me with a possible concussion, it sounded crazy.

"Well, can't say that's the first time I've heard that one." His laugh was as deep as his voice. "We are on the E.T. Highway and Area 51 is right by the mountains."

I settled back into the seat of his truck, pulled on my seatbelt as he did a U-turn, and headed back toward Las Vegas. "It was definitely an ugly little green man."

Chapter 4

1800s: KINGSTOWN, IRELAND

Seagulls dive-bombed the beacon top of the East Pier Lighthouse, the dome creating an easy target. Elmville dodged the creamy, slimy, gooey droppings as he headed inside, breathing through his hawk-like nose to avoid inhaling the fishy odor.

He'd developed great upper-body strength as a leprechaun. Good thing, since he had to pull himself up and over obstacles way too many times. Despite his planning and blueprint reading, he had one problem area he couldn't avoid.

Whistling preceded said problem as the lighthouse keeper appeared on its stairs, pulled a brass pocket watch from his uniform, glanced at it, and began to light the lanterns. Elmville watched through the multi-windowed structure as the man went about his business. The intensity of the lights blinded him as the mechanism rotated.

Finished with his duty, the lighthouse keeper stomped down the staircase, his whistling growing more distant with every footfall.

Elmville heard the ground-level door close before he opened every other lantern, and turned down the wicks, dimming the powerful lights. He too whistled as he continued his task, his breath becoming labored after his exertion. Tiredness crept in as the night crept on. At last, he climbed down from the final lantern and slid down the railing to the bottom of the lighthouse. Finding a comfortable spot behind a stained mailbag, he slept.

****

Waves battled the steamship Victoria as Susan Tobin gripped the handrail, counting the stars to get her mind off her heaving stomach. Focusing on the reunion with her parents, did nothing to tame the queasiness. Whitecaps crashed against the hull of the vessel, splashing her in their intensity. Her dress now drenched and transparent, she grasped onto the only valuable item on her body—her necklace. She wiped the water from her face and grabbed onto a rope to keep her feet planted, the railing now too slippery, too greased to gain purchase.

She sighted William, her brother at the other end of the ship, as he weaved toward her.

The rope coiled around her leg, and as she attempted to untangle herself, it only tightened. She screamed for help, but her pleas were silenced by the wind. The ship heaved and rolled to the left. She grappled for purchase on the deck, but slick with Dublin Bay water, there was nothing left to anchor her.

"Sister, grab ahold of the railing," William bellowed, his words stolen by the wind.

Panicked, she snatched at her necklace, a gift from her brother, the chain now broken, the locket skittering across the drenched deck. She was suddenly airborne as she fell overboard. The twisted rope broke the fall but now tightened around her throat, an unforgiving noose.

****

Elmville was awakened by a thud. He observed a bundle of freshly printed newspapers thrown beside the mailbag. Commotion from gulls screeching overhead surrounded the lighthouse, but the lighthouse keeper was no longer whistling. As he unfolded one of the newspapers, his face went as white as the excretion from the seagulls.

"Two Ships collided—twenty lives lost, including our own Susan Tobin." The lighthouse keeper read the headline aloud.

A cold northerly wind rustled the pages, flipping the sheets, before stopping at the obituaries.

Elmville scanned the names, settling back to read the one he was most interested in.

Susan Tobin (1838-1872)

As the result of a tragic shipwreck, we lost our dear Susan. The town is left to mourn her death, her body recovered from the wreckage. May the Irish hills caress you. May her lakes and rivers bless you. May the luck of the Irish enfold you. Saint Patrick behold you.

She leaves behind her beloved brother William as well as her parents Edith and Donal Tobin. God Speed Susan.

Elmville grinned. "Onward and upward!"

Chapter 5

KITTY: NOW

"So your CT scan came back okay?" Ben asked as he tucked his legs under my Elvis blanket, a cup of Earl Grey tea in his hands.

"Yes, Fred took me to emergency and they ran a scan. The doctor said no bleeding or swelling, just a bit of whiplash, and to just ice, if needed." I sipped my tea. "Cripes, you think I'd know enough to wait at least five minutes when you offer to make me tea. I burned my tongue." I threw the blanket off and headed into my minuscule kitchen, grabbing an ice cube from the freezer. I rubbed it on my tongue to dull the pain, before dropping it into the tea cup.

My casita was the one good thing in my life. Okay, it was on my mom's property, but I had my own separate living accommodation in Las Vegas—okay, North Las Vegas but even so, something to be proud of. Bookcases lined every wall, and even inside the kitchen cupboards were books. In addition, I made a little lending library outside for the neighbors.

Ben called it my granny flat, but I loved how it was all on one level and had everything I needed. I had two separate bedrooms—not that mine ever got any action other than if I was having a particularly vigorous dream—my own washer and dryer and a table for my puzzles. What more could I ask for? And yes, I paid rent.

"Tell me all about the latest mystery man," I asked, living vicariously through Ben and his love life.

"Kitty, I have to tell you, he has it all. He was as cute as could be, had an accent to die for and Smokey curled up in his lap." Ben had a dreamy look in his eyes, like they were glazed over. Almost the stare I had when I went into Smith's Grocery store and saw a tray of their cherry fritters.

"Smokey doesn't like anyone, even me. I have the scratches to prove it." I held out my arm in evidence.

"She is a good judge of character. Only kidding." Ben laughed as I yanked the blanket off him. "Seriously though, Kitty, I thought he was the one. I had butterflies, the flutters. It was like I was home." Ben sighed. "But I guess what happens in Vegas, stays in Vegas. Even though we didn't get into tops or bottoms, just some kissing. Mostly talking." Ben stopped talking when I held up my hand. "Right, TMI."

"I'm glad you found *the one,*" I said, and I was generally happy for my BFF. Why couldn't I find *the one or even the one right now*?

The last guy who cradled me was Fred at my accident, and he was married—with kids.

"I don't want to rub salt into the wound. I know you'll find your Mr. Right, but back to me, he hasn't called or sent a text. There's been zero follow-up." He shrugged. "I guess I was the only one who had the butterflies. As they say, it's better to have loved and lost."

"It was one night." Ben was dramatic and wore his heart on his sleeve. He once thought he and an order taker from a local burger restaurant shared a look. He must have dragged me through the drive-through twenty times before he got up the nerve to ask the guy out. It wasn't a pretty rejection, but the fact Smokey liked this guy was something new. Ben never took his dates home.

"Switching topics, will you help me?" Ben asked, removing his Covid mask to sip the tea before slipping it back on.

I slid my Sudoku book away from his reach as he's been known to fill in the wrong numbers with the same pen I used. He was a pain, always had been and always will be.

"You're telling me, Mom and I get to go to Ireland for free because your mom has Covid and you have to stay home and look after her." I wanted to dig deeper, but with Ben, I was more afraid of what the downside was because, with Ben, there was always something. He was a great friend, a good wingman when we did venture to the Strip, except we were honing in on the same species, and more often than not, the species were interested in him and not me.

"Yep, that's it. I can't leave Mom, you know, Covid and the elderly. It's her bucket list to go to Ireland to meet her relatives, but we'll have to make it another time." Ben sipped his tea, and I picked up my Elvis cup, remembering to blow on the liquid before taking a sip. My tongue stung, but I took one for the team.

"So, there's no hidden agenda and we get to stay in a castle." The cover of my current read sat open on the coffee table, a castle and knight prominent.

"Yep, that's it. One of you can fly in first class but

the other, in the back of the plane." Ben picked up the book, checked out the knight, then replaced the book, removing my bookmark. "Oops, sorry about that. Hope you remember where you were."

"I'm okay with that." I'd learned in my years of knowing Ben, it was a trait of his to be annoying, and I always kept track of where I was in a book, if I knew he was coming over. "Mom deserves a treat after what she's been through this year."

"What a daughter you are!" Ben gulped down the rest of his tea. "I must head back to work. Lunch hours are never an hour when Chas is in the house." Ben is a personal assistant and I've become skilled at tuning out his complaints about his boss. I can only hear so many times about how anal the guy is about matching socks and his thousand-dollar shoes.

"Thanks for dropping by." I carried my tea to the door, placed it on the hall table, then gave him a massive hug. "And thanks for the trip."

Mom pulled into the breezeway and stepped out of the loaner car she'd rented while our car was in the body shop. "Ben, thanks so much. Kitty told me about your generosity. I'm sorry your mom isn't well. This Covid is really something. I got a shot. I know it's not the popular thing to do, but I figure they did testing, and who knows what kind of testing they are doing at Area 51." Mom chuckled.

"Very true, Annie. I wished you would talk my mom into getting the jab. Then I'd be on my way to the Emerald Isle and you two would be stuck here."

"Is there anything we need to know?" Mom asked Ben as she lugged bags from the mall off the front seat. "I had to get some new clothes for our trip. I heard it's a little cooler over there than here, so I needed sweaters and a cute rain jacket. Do you know how hard it is to find a raincoat in Vegas?"

"I'm sure you succeeded in your mission, Mom."

"I did, and I found the cutest sweatshirt with Harvard on it for you."

"Mom, I'm not fourteen. You don't need to buy me clothes. I'm capable of buying my own." Sometimes Mom just set my teeth on edge. "I'm twenty-four years old."

"Kitty, your mom did something nice. Let it go," Ben said, unlocking the door of his Kia. "You should see the stuff my mom buys me. The t-shirts have so much bling you could light the Vegas Strip."

"The road to hell is paved with good intentions," Mom chimed in as she hauled the bags inside her house.

"Oh, before I forget, I've emailed you the tickets and info on the hotel. He's going to be there as well, there's a Bitcoin convention he wants to attend."

"Who is he?"

"Chas! Toodles."

Chapter 6

DRURIE: NOW

"Drurie, King Cloverdale is demanding to see you!" Elmville whined, his nasally voice gritted on my nerves like an elm branch rubbing against withered bark. Very annoying.

"I thought you were away on vacation, across the pond. Besides, I'll talk to him later. I'm just on my way out."

"I didn't know you kept track of my comings and goings, bro, but you don't seem to understand—he wants to see you now and you are to accompany me." He grabbed me by my green velvet jacket, popping one of the golden cuff buttons off onto the dirt floor. I yanked my arm away from him and retrieved the button. "You're going to pay to have this repaired."

"Yeah, that's if you live that long," Elmville snickered and snorted through his bulbous nose.

Shiny double doors flanked the roots of the elm tree, oblivious to all the humans but obvious to forest dwellers. With a slight touch, the doors opened, and I strutted through with confidence I didn't feel. I didn't want to show Elmville my inner turmoil at being summoned by the high commander.

"Better you than me, buddy. I bet you're still in trouble over the potato famine. What an epic screw-up that was." Elmville rubbed his Shenandoah beard. "Oh, I think I'll cause a little mischief and see what happens when I put this fungus on a potato leaf. Major fail. See you, see you, wouldn't want to be you."

"Yeah, well, at least I don't have my head up the king's butt so far that I can see out his nose," I said, wishing I could thwack my shillelagh over the head of this annoying being. It didn't matter he was my brother, my younger brother in fact, by several hundred years. Blood, in this case, was not thicker than water. In fact, I would kill him in a hummingbird's heartbeat without a second thought, but what I had in my heart wasn't in my head. I was passive by nature, a tree hugger if you will, but it didn't mean I hadn't thought of it. The more gruesome the better, but again, one cannot be arrested and tried for one's thoughts. If that was the case, well, the prisons would already be overcrowded more than they are.

I stumbled over the roots of the tree and continued down the dirt hallway accented by bottle-green ferns. Trickles of sunlight nudged through the gaps in the bark. Faintly, the sound of dripping water became a backdrop to the haven. All too soon we reached the end, only to be presented with another set of doors, these opened by a chain of ants, the top being at doorknob height. It swung open.

Sunlight shone brighter here, and a glow fell on the throne of the king. Every time I entered his chamber, which thankfully wasn't all that often, I was awestruck by the simpleness yet regency it commanded. A simple tree trunk had been carved by woodpeckers into clovers, each one more feather-like than the last. It was the intricacy of the designs that impressed me. I daren't reach up to touch them, fearing the lace-like facets would fall apart in my hand. A pump organ sat against one wall, confusing me with how they managed to get such a large piece through the smallish doors. I turned my attention away from them only to have my glance fall onto the throne itself. It was carved from Carboniferous Limestone, the seat and backrest chiseled out while the arms worn smooth and flanked into scepters green Connemara marble. When the summer solstice shone through the slits in the bark, it was a sight to behold. I had only seen it once in my numerous lifetimes, but it was something you never forgot.

"Welcome, Drurie. You can go now, Elmville." King Cloverdale's voice boomed through the trunk of the tree, his presence commanding the squirrels and chipmunks to quiver as they perched on their back legs and arranged their nuts in precision rows.

"Are you sure, sir? I can stay if you need my assistance. I know how difficult Drurie can be at times." Elmville removed his tri-peaked hat and bowed.

"Do you not think I can handle your brother? I asked you to leave, as this does not concern you." With a dismissive wave, he waited until Elmville lumbered out of the antechamber before he continued. "Everyone has a cross to bear." He chuckled as a deep-throated cough resonated through his words. "And he obviously is yours."

"You got that right, sir. I didn't appreciate the first hundred years of my life when I only had three hundred siblings. Funny how one can be such a pain." I smiled as if I was jesting, but alas, I was not.

The King coughed into the sleeve of his golden

velvet jacket, a string of phlegm trailing from his mouth to the jacket.

"Please, have a seat." He pointed to the wooden chair, detailed with three-dimensional multi-colored rainbows, mating unicorns, and cardinals painted in vibrant reds and browns sourced from berries, leaves, and forest flowers.

I did as I was told and sat on the side. The seat was comfortable, but my anxiety put me on edge. My palms were moist and I could feel sweat dripping down my back. Despite the calmness I relayed to my brother, I didn't like to be called to the king's office, and I did feel bad about the potato famine, but in the words of kids everywhere. It wasn't my fault.

"I will keep this short and please come closer as the walls have ears and I don't want this to go any further than the two of us." He waved me closer as he leaned forward on the throne. I was close enough to smell his peppermint-laden breath, hoping at the same time he couldn't smell the odor lingering on mine.

"This is what I need you to do. When you accomplish it, all will be forgiven with the famine fiasco."

My eyes widened as I registered the enormity of what he was explaining as the ants created various shapes in their chain. I almost lost my train of thought as the ants created seahorses and mermaids. Where in the heck would a colony of ants see a seahorse or mermaid? It boggled the mind, but I had to pay attention to what King Cloverdale was outlining. Forgiveness for the famine! Though, I still didn't know how the spore ended up in my pocket.

As he finished, a loud clap of thunder broke the air

and startled me out of the chair, and I fell onto the dirt floor. On the left side of the antechamber was the pump organ, which began to play by itself. My eyebrows shot up in surprise, the greenish hue draining out of my skin as when I looked at my hand, it was as white as a dove. King Cloverdale shrugged his shoulders. "I keep telling Elmville it needs to get fixed, but I guess he has bigger fish to fry."

I should have guessed my brother would have had a hand in scaring the greenness out of me.

"Off with you and I will need updates as to your success. Remember, you are the one I entrust with this, but it must be kept confidential so your effects are not sabotaged."

In a trance, I retraced my path back the way I came, though now somewhat staggering with the enormity of the events that rested on my shoulders.

A pixie with the most beautiful monarch butterfly wings spoke as I exited the tree. "Kind, sir, your chariot awaits." She waved her wings tauntingly as though impatient, setting their golds and yellows to shimmer in the sunlight poking through the water-laden clouds. I knew from experience we were about to be rained upon momentarily.

"Am I waiting for your partner in crime or are you venturing out on your own today?" she asked.

"Duncan, are you coming?" I tapped my shillelagh three times against the bark of our elm tree, waiting with extreme patience as I watched beautiful wings dancing back and forth, hither and yon with hypnotic effect.

Her strident tone cut through my admiring haze. "I don't mean to be a dragon downer, but if I'm going to get you to Whitestone Castle before the rain, we have to get a move on. Tempus fugit and all that."

Without hesitation, I climbed onto her back and tucked my shillelagh against my thigh.

"Wait, wait, I'm coming." I glanced behind me to see my best mate and cousin, Duncan, race out the door. I cringed as he slammed it, knowing when we returned there would be hell to pay with King Cloverdale. He lived for peace and quiet, which is quite ironic considering how he spent his days, in charge of hundreds of leprechauns, and that was just my immediate family.

"Sorry for the delay. I was in conference with Elmville and you know how he likes to go on and on about nothing."

"What are you wasting your time with him for?" I made room for Duncan on the pixie's back. As he settled in behind me, he too seemed to lose his train of thought as he watched her wings."Wow, aren't they something?"

"I agree, but you were speaking about Elmville." I tucked my knees gently into her mandibles, not wanting to hurt her at all, but I really didn't want to fall off and embarrass myself. Duncan would never let me live it down and since we leprechauns live to a ripe old age, I didn't want to hear about it literally forever.

Pixie tucked her wings and began a downward spiral. I hung onto my tri-sided hat with my left hand and my shillelagh with my right. It was my favorite hat and I'd be darned if I would bother Pixie to do a dive-bomb to retrieve it. I felt a tap on my shoulder. Duncan pointed down at his shillelagh, which was spiraling faster than an ash key on a blustery day.

Pixie glanced over her shoulder and gave him *the look*. She reversed course and dipsy doodled toward the escapee. It became a game as the wind was playing at keeping it away from us. My stomach was not sitting well with the jerking and jolting motions. I have somewhat sensitive innards, something I know leprechauns aren't known for, more so for the frolicking around and making rainbows and unicorns but I digress.

Pixie shifted her wings into overdrive and we naturally tucked our bodies down to make it easier for her to streamline the course. Downward we traveled in our attempt to intercept the shillelagh before it did any damage to anyone or anything below us. Once upon a time, I neglected to secure mine and it thwacked a sheep on the noggin. The sheep was never the same. Though, how can you tell with sheep, but I did witness it giving a high yield of wool that year, not that I'm taking credit but one must do what one can do.

Oh, fiddle sticks!!!

Chapter 7

May Day
KINGSTOWN, IRELAND

Children dressed in white, adorned with yellow flowers in their hair, grabbed ribbons, the older children stealing from the younger ones to dance around the May pole as adults formed an improper circle, gossiping. A pipe band of bagpipers played "My Home," the adults clapping along to the beat.

Elmville clambered down from the knot in an oak tree, heading toward the train station. Normally busy with travelers, all who were attending May Day celebrations were already in Kingstown, and if they weren't, too bad, too sad.

Tongue stuck in the side of his cheek, he began painting the rail tracks with whale oil stolen from the East Pier Lighthouse. It was all he could do to keep his lunch down as the smell of the oil invaded his nostrils. "My Home" stuck in his head like a bad earworm. He hummed as he covered miles of the track with the oil, the band providing the backdrop with the music. Finally satisfied, he plopped down on his butt and surveyed his work.

Despite the holiday, the cattle train was on time to the yards, the livestock ready in preparation for auction. In the distance, Elmville saw the lone light and heard the clickity clack of the wheels. A distant mooing filled the background.

Approaching the station and nearing the town, the conductor attempted to engage the brakes; the squealing of the handbrake, all futile. The train purged onward, the smoke billowing from the stack.

Movement in Elmville's peripheral vision distracted him from the train. A Clouded Yellow butterfly, its pale shading almost a translucent white, fluttered and flowed across the tracks, stopping to rest on the lavender plant adjacent to the railway ties.

"Sarah Tobin, where are you?" a distant panicky voice called out as a child dressed in white, with a variety of colored ribbons in her hair, stepped through the doors of the station, and enamored by the butterfly, watched spellbound.

Sucking in his breath, Elmville kept the butterfly on the plant, overriding its urge to take flight.

Sarah jumped down off of the station platform and skittered over to the stagnant butterfly, its wings dancing a slow and mesmerizing waltz.

The train's light grew brighter and a horn sounded, but Sarah ignored all, as she reached out to pet the butterfly.

Elmville continued to inhale. The butterfly remained where it was as Sarah stroked the insect with the care and attention that a new mother would give an infant.

"Sarah, no!!!" A mother screeched, her focus on the girl and not realizing the height of the step down caught her shoe on the railroad tie. She hobbled toward the girl, her white as a Trillium flowered dress bellowing in the fresh springtime air.

A smile encrusted the girl's face as she pointed toward the butterfly, her locket catching the sun, the glare distracting, blinding the train engineer.

Unable to hold his breath any longer, Elmville let out a wheeze, and the butterfly rose, fluttering into the crosswind, the humans pivoting to watch the spectacle as a Red Admiral butterfly joined and they flew in sequence.

Jolted, the mother grabbed the girl out of harm's way as the train approached, its cattle catcher mere seconds away. The girl squirmed, twisting to continue watching the butterflies in flight, oblivious to the train.

Clouds of black plumes billowed from the engine as the engineer frantically pulled the cord, sounding the whistle. Elmville saw the operator push back his cap and close his eyes, bracing for the impact. Elmville stuck his knobby fingers in his ears as the train screeched, and a foot flew past his head, his reflex to duck. Ribbons, formally in Sarah's hair, now cascaded onto the cattle catcher at the front of the train, like a macabre bunting, gently blowing in the noonday breeze.

Blood poured from all orifices of the crushed bodies. The girl's dress ripped and torn now was stained red, and the mother's body parts were strewn hither and yon. Her head rolled beside him. Her face was a mixture of horror and peace. One eye was bloodied and closed, the other open wide as if still watching the butterflies in flight.

Elmville clapped his hands and did the Leprechaunjot. The train now stopped, the middle cattle car at his sight level. He stood eye to eye with a bovine. The heifer shook its head back and forth, drool slithering from its mouth as it pawed at the cage, seemingly wanting to get to Elmville.

Sticking his tongue out at the cow, he ran back to the festivities, his task for the day completed. He would celebrate by chowing down on candied apples and cotton candy as only a leprechaun could.

Chapter 8

KITTY: NOW

"He's not here." Mom stopped suddenly in the arrivals area of Dublin Airport, Chas L. Brownridge stepping on her left heel as I peeked inside the file Ben had so conveniently left on my front step this morning. Coward that he was, he wouldn't answer my phone calls, texts, or front door when I went to his apartment. Really, I didn't want to kill him, only to ask him a few questions.

But Mom and I could figure it out without him. We'd been on our own without a male figure for a long time. We've got this.

The man she was referring to was on page one. We were to meet a driver holding a sign with our name on it at the arrivals area.

"Mom! What's going on? Didn't Ben arrange for someone to be here?" Mom didn't need to turn to witness my eye rolling and glaring as only Gen Z'ers have been trained to do. Ben, while he wasn't answering me, was on daily group chats with Mom.

"You should have arranged it better, checked and double-checked." Chas held his phone aloft in one hand, while he ran the other through his chocolate brown curly hair.

"I did, and I have the emails to prove it. Here,

look!" Mom thumbed through, prepared to present them as defense. "Ben said he arranged everything."

"It's not Mom's fault if the guy isn't here." Wait!! It was okay for me to pick on Mom but not this jerk."Maybe you should just take a chill pill."

"Kitty, please don't talk to Chas in that tone. We don't want to make things worse for Ben."

"Right. While you two sat in Business Class, I was back with the peasants in steerage. Stuffed like a pepper, I couldn't even stretch my legs." I grimaced as pain shot up my leg. I vented. "Wow, what a fun time stuck beside an overweight bald guy who farted every time he shifted position. I don't think I can breathe anymore. I should have brought my thicker Covid mask. At least it would have covered the smell. And noise. It sounded like the fighter jets flying over our place in Vegas from Nellis Air Force Base. This is what he gave me." I handed my mother a drawing of a leprechaun beside a donkey. "Great, just what I want to remember my airplane trip to Hell. A little green man and an ass."

My mother struggled to cover her laugh as I continued my rant. "Don't get me started on the grandmother who wanted my phone number to give to her catch of a grandson. He was cute in the picture, but then she proceeded to fall asleep on my shoulder and drooled on my top, which is Chloe's, by the way. Who knows if she'll ever speak to me again when she sees the curry stain! What grandmother eats curry on the plane? That's just a recipe for heading to the can, which I had to share with forty other people because my butt can't sit on the can in first class. But as long as you and Charlie are happy and rested, well, that's the main thing, isn't it?" I was *sooo* mad at Ben. I knew I had to sit in the back of the plane, but really, there wasn't even a food package, and I couldn't figure out how to work the television, so I watched commercials for the entire flight. Even the flight attendant couldn't figure out the television.

He'd ordered himself the bare bones seat, so his mother could sit beside Chas in business class. What a guy! Wait, knowing Ben as I did, he'd be flirting with the flight attendants in business while his mom was at the back. Yes, more like it. Just wait, my friend, until I'm on Vegas soil.

"Dear, you should have come and got me. I would have switched seats with you." Mom smiled, suddenly concerned. "Are your headaches acting up again, from the car accident?"

"My headaches are almost gone now. The doctor just said to monitor them. Sure, now you decide to become maternal." I couldn't help blasting my mom. Sometimes it was just way too easy, so I continued. "I thought we were helping out Ben, but I'm in Ireland where it rains continually and I can't eat French fries."

"Sorry, why can't she eat French fries? What did I miss?" Chas asked, glancing back to his phone, before reaching into the inside pocket of his suit jacket.

"Duh, for someone who is supposed to be so educated, you haven't heard of the potato famine, where the country relied on potatoes and starved to death." I let out a loud sigh, which I'm sure could be heard back in Las Vegas, at the very least by the disembarking passengers.

"She does know it was hundreds of years ago?" Chas addressed Mom, ignoring me, an infuriating habit

I noticed he had. In one of his many rants, Ben admitted Chas was very condescending, and apparently, he was like that to everyone.

"She does know, but she is not taking any chances," Mom agreed while I glared. I pulled my long acorn-colored hair into a ponytail with the elastic band I constantly wore on my right wrist. I shifted the straps of my backpack further onto my shoulders.

I attempted to get cell, text, or anything to reach Ben as he failed to provide a follow-up number for the driving service. *Ben, you really dropped the ball.*

Mom's eyes surveyed the crowd, searching feverishly for the sign.

"Oh, geez! I'm not getting into this in front of *him*." Chas did not need to know my mother thought I was a) ready for the psych ward,b) a drug addict, and/or c) I had a brain tumor brought on by the airbags. I erred when I told her what I had seen in my headlights. I should have kept my mouth shut, but no, in the manner of sharing, I blurted out about the little green man.

The grandmother who I sat beside on the plane happened to walk by just as I spoke and the scowl on her face, well I didn't have to know her history, which I did, to know she was a mother. She had the look down perfectly."Sorry, no offense, but I'm sure your country is lovely. I mean, it has a rock people kiss so they can talk more. How can a country be bad? Just not my cup of tea, especially with Covid so recent and all."

"You, young lady, should not make fun of superstitions, and you are not going anywhere," Chas said, watching me eyeing the reservations desk as at the same time he grabbed my wrist. I could pay for myself to go back to Vegas and throttle Ben sooner rather than later.

"Let go of me." I twirled around and tugged away from his steel grip, my elbow shot out and his phone flew across the floor of the airport, glass from the screen shattering in the wake of destruction.

"Look, you ungrateful sod. Do you know how much that phone is worth? You'll be buying me a new one, so forget about a ticket home. Your money is going to fix my phone." He bent to pick up the phone and ignored the glass fragments on the floor. What a jerk. Anyone could step on them and cut themselves if they were in flip-flops. Okay, so I was, and I so could. They are comfy to travel in.

"Isn't it a work phone?" I asked as I bent to pick up the glass, and ended up on my butt, the hem of my sundress catching as a crowd gathered and cell phones zoomed in. Great! I was going to go viral and not in a good way.

"Chas, it was an accident. She didn't mean to break your phone. Come on, Kitty, apologize, and let's look for our driver."

If you hadn't guessed by now, my mother was the peacekeeper in any situation, though it didn't make Dad want to stay with us.

"Sorry," I whispered, not meaning it by any stretch of the imagination, but anything to make the crowd and the phones go away.

Chas squeezed my mom's shoulder hard and her skin turned red, the area already beginning to bruise. "I believe you sent emails to Ben and all, but it doesn't change the result. We're here at the airport and there's no one holding a sign with our name on it. As a result of the incompetence, whether yours or his, we're going to be late checking into the hotel and miss the drinks." He patted my mom on the head like she was a dog who couldn't learn to fetch, a gesture beyond condescending. Her five-foot-four frame barely reached his shoulder. "I'll be right back. I'm going to head into Boots to pick up some gifts and see if I can get a new phone."

"Is he buying gifts for his staff? I don't think Ben is on the list," I couldn't resist asking my mom.

Ignoring my comment, she glanced around the terminal, looking for a four-leaf clover in a field of grass.

Chas left his carry-on with us, and without a backward glance, headed into the store. The minute he entered, the salesgirl flocked to him like a homing pigeon and he was her messenger.

"Show's over folks." I pulled myself up, stubbing my toe kicking his luggage, and again glanced toward the arrivals. Posh limo drivers outfitted with caps and suits held up professionally lettered signs, some even on tablets, patiently waiting for their charges. There was a flurry of activity, pushing and shoving on the left side of the rope barrier. A brown cardboard sign, creased in the middle and stained at the top left with what looked like ketchup, or was part of a very bloody murder scene? Written across it was Castle Whitestone.

"Oh, frig. Look, Kitty, there he is." In my mom's attempt to wave and get his attention, she grabbed the suitcases, only to have Chas' tip over onto her foot, knocking her to the cold linoleum floor. Maybe I shouldn't make fun of superstitions.

The sign holder bolted under the rope, kneeling beside Mom. "Mamam, are you okay? I feel this is my fault. I'm sorry I'm late. I had an emergency. Do you mind? Let me know if this hurts." Instantly, his hand was on her ankle and he began to massage it, monitoring the pain in her eyes while he carefully put pressure on different points.

"What are you doing? Don't you lay a hand on her!" Chas' voice boomed as he set his purchases down on the floor but didn't approach.

"He's helping me. Your luggage fell on my foot." Helped up by the sign holder, Mom couldn't put any weight on her ankle as he struggled to stand her upright. With a high-pitched whistle, he waved toward a porter, who had a wheelchair, and poured Mom in. I think she liked the attention from our driver.

"My luggage is hardly to be blamed for your clumsiness. Now, can we get going? I hope you're not parked too far away. This luggage is heavy and these wheels are somewhat useless." Chas led the way, arrogantly bumping his way through the crowd. "Kitty, can you manage the luggage? Probably the least you can do," Chas asked, not waiting for an answer as he dumped the bags on top of Mom's lap, leaving Chas to handle his phone, and me the luggage.

"Man, he's a piece of work," the sign holder/driver muttered as he hooked the baggage handles onto the arms of the wheelchair and pushed Mom through the sliding doors and out into the traffic lane before crossing into the carpark.

As we approached a blue Audi, a white dog jumped from the passenger seat to the driver's, then back again, barking ferociously before recognizing our driver. I could see the tail wagging like a windshield wiper on high through the window.

"Just a sec and I'll unlock the doors. I just have to grab the dog to make sure she doesn't get out." Concerned for Mom, he continued, "Mamam, are you okay to lean against the car while I open the door?"

"Yes, of course." She pushed herself up from the comfort of the wheelchair and hobbled toward the front of the car, sending the dog into rapture. Mom wasn't totally helpless, and he was kinda cute, the guy and the dog.

He grabbed the dog's leash and pulled the dog out, wiping down the dog hair. "Sorry, I thought there were only two people I was picking up, but not to worry, the more the merrier."

"Ben is so disorganized. There were always three." Chas rapidly texted into his phone. "I don't know why I put up with him. There are so many more competent assistants out there."

I don't think I could put up with this arse. Ireland or not, I was really considering heading back home. Mom, my facial expression expert, could read me like a cereal box.

"Kitty, can we drop it, please? You are not going home, and that's the end of the discussion." Mom flipped through the folder like it was the Holy Grail.

"Are you not a fan of our fair country?" the driver asked me as he settled Mom into the back seat. "Would you mind holding the leash for a moment while I load the luggage into the boot?" The dog glanced from the driver to me, then promptly lifted one leg and peed on the tire closest to Chas.

"I've nothing against your country. It's my mother I have the beef with. I'm twenty-four years old and she still mothers me."

"Gotcha. Well, mothers tend to do that. My dad has a friend whose mother still calls him to ensure he got home from the pub okay and he's in his seventies, which makes her in her late eighties." He laughed when he witnessed the look on my face. "But no worries. We're going to have to win you over. Between the leprechauns and the pots of gold, it shouldn't be too hard."

"Sure, short little green men with attitudes, like I don't already have enough of those in my life." I glanced toward Chas who was ignoring us as he settled inside the car behind the passenger seat.

The driver pushed the seat as far back as it would go, forcing Chas to origami his legs. My mom had considerably more room as I turned to see her right knee knocking against the oversized burgundy luggage that wouldn't fit in the car's boot.

Following the arrows through the carpark, he paid and then headed through three roundabouts in succession, before heading out of the city onto a two-lane highway, surrounded by fields.

The dog sat contently on my lap, tartan collared, on high alert with her paws on the dash, where at home I'd have my bare feet, something that drove my mother to distraction.

"What's your dog's name again?" Mom asked as I saw her glance at the license affixed to the dashboard in plastic, "Coyne."

"The name of my wee dog is Madigan, which in Celtic means small dog." He turned to grin at Mom, his blue eyes the same shade as the sky outside the window, crinkled and dimples dug deep into his cheeks. Wow, what a specimen. He definitely had the Colin

Firth vibe going on. Actually, I was becoming impressed with what Ireland had to offer. I might have to stay to see how this all played out. Go, Mom!

The Audi crept along the single-lane gravel road, bordered by fields crisscrossed by stone fences. The vehicle stopped as a flock of sheep—boredom etched on their faces—ambled across the road.

"Really!! How much longer is this going to take?" Chas sighed."Doesn't a car have the right of way over a herd of sheep? What kind of country is this? This would never happen in America." He drew a deep breath and returned his attention to his phone. "I have an important phone call I must take in ten minutes and I can't get any frigging cell service. My eyes are going to be crossed when I'm finally able to read my emails."

"Coyne, is there any way you can get Chas a signal?" Mom asked, not above using her feminine charms to make life easier for Chas and for herself. It was second nature for her to coddle a man. My father had it good, but it still didn't keep him out from between the legs of a showgirl. My future step-mom was five years older than me. Tonight would not be pleasant if Chas was in a bad mood and therefore, my night would not be enjoyable. I intended to enjoy as much of Ireland as I could in the short time we would be here, now I've had a good look at Coyne. He might not be boyfriend material, but he looked like he knew the right end of a Guinness.

"I'll give it a lash." Coyne glanced at the clock on the dashboard and gave a small wave to the shepherd as he lowered the window. The scent of sheep's wool, manure, and the freshness of freshly cut grass filled the car. "Finn, are we on tonight? Eight at the Leprechaun's

Door?"

Finn sauntered over to the door and leaned in the window. "Grand. I'll need a team for the Trivia, are you game? Flossy has to stay at the barn and babysit." He peered into the car. "Looks like we have some new blood."

"Kitty, you always like trivia. She's really good at Jeopardy." Mom leaned forward into the front seat and petted the dog.

"Mom, I'm not going to play trivia," I announced, petting the dog as Mom glanced at the shepherd. He had the Tom Holland hair going on and it appeared one didn't need to spend time in the gym if you herded sheep.

"Well, that's a shame. You don't look like a minus craic, but I don't want to force you if you're too scared to represent your county against us foreigners." He saluted and continued on his way, his staff gently prodding his flock as his Austrian Shepherd dog nudged the stragglers.

"What's the Leprechaun's Door?" I asked as the car came to a standstill while we waited for the sheep to pass. Wait, what? What did he just call me?

"How old is she?" Coyne turned to ask my mom, his eyes twinkling. "He said minus craic, basically a person who is no fun."

"She is twenty-four," I answered indigently. "And she could speak for herself since she was four, and she is a fun person."

"Actually, it was three when you spoke your first word," Mom said proudly as if she had anything to do with it.

"I bet it was 'not,'" Chas said, "or probably

definitely 'no'".

I turned and stuck my tongue out at him, but he couldn't see me since he was directly behind me.

"Believe it or not, her first word was potato, except she pronounced it, pot at o."

"Nothing wrong with that. She spoke it in the manner of the true Irish. Is there Irish in your blood?" Coyne asked, as he leaned over to pet his dog, and dug a treat out the side pocket of the car door, and handed it to me to give to Madison. "Now she'll be your friend for life."

"She's pretty easy to bribe." I laughed, feeling content for the first time in weeks. "But what is the Leprechaun's Door? Now you've decided I'm past the age of consent."

"Meet me in the lobby at seven, and dress comfortably. I'll take you the easy way, so it won't be too difficult with your foot." He addressed my mom, not me.

"I'm undecided about the trivia. My mom can use a cane, they're for old people."

"Or leprechauns," Coyne said with a wayward grin.

"Not even in the country for two hours and already you have a date." My mom clapped her hands seal-like.

"It's not a date," Coyne and I said in unison.

Chapter 9

ANNIE: NOW

"These stone fences are so cute." Annie clicked pictures with her phone, immediately forwarding them to Kitty. "Kitty, I just sent you some pics. Chas, look at what you're missing."

"Mom, you know we can't get cell service, so don't send me any pictures." Geez. Mom could be so smart in some ways and totally clueless in others. Was she even aware of Coyne's attention?

"Imagine how sore their backs must be every day laying over eighteen feet of wall. Unbelievable to think of how long it took them to create all these. There are tens of thousands of miles of these walls. Definitely no acting like a maggot—sorry, messing around." Coyne waved his arms to take in the expanse of the area. As far as the eye could see there were the stone fences. "If you look closely at the stones as well, you'll see birds' nests in between the rocks in addition to moss, which attaches itself to the rocks. The mycophiles have a field day. There's a real ecosystem in these stones." Pride controlled his words.

"Sorry, what's a mycophile?"Annie asked, not afraid to show her ignorance in front of Kitty or Chas.

His Irish drawl drew out the word. "Mycophile— mushroom pickers. There are some of the rarest mushrooms here, but you have to know what you're picking as some are poisonous. Many a king has been laid to rest coming in at the wrong end of one." He shifted gears before adding, "If that question gets asked in trivia, you'll know the answer."

"True that! Amazing!! I'll be sure not to eat anything without your approval." Annie continued to take pictures."And all the shades of green, imagine seeing this every day. Do you ever get bored?"

"There's a famous Irish saying: There are only two kinds of people in the world, those who are Irish and those who wish they were."

"Why would you want to live in a place where it rains all the time?" Kitty asked as she petted the dog. Despite her annoyance with, well, everything, Annie grinned back, knowing if he was listening, it would be getting Chas' goat or sheep. If he couldn't see it, he didn't regard it as being real. She had learned so much about the man during the flight.

"That I don't doubt," Chas muttered.

"I have, but that's a conversation for another day." Coyne reached over and petted his dog. "Shall I continue?"

"Please do." Annie closed her eyes, his voice transporting her to another time and place. She could listen to his accent all day long as Kitty nodded.

"Sir, you should be able to get a signal once I get to the top of the hill, just past the sheep. Castle Whitestone was orientally built in 1067 from wood dragged from the bogs nearby. When a fire engulfed the entire building, it was later reconstructed of local stone," Coyne explained, glancing over his left shoulder.

"Wow, they were none too bright back in the day,

were they?" Chas snickered. Catching the exasperated looks from everyone in the car, he continued, "Annie, they make fires out of logs. It doesn't take a brain surgeon to realize a fire might happen if you make your house of wood. Look at the three little pigs." He laughed to himself and began typing feverishly on his phone, an offline game filling the screen.

"Please continue, Coyne. I find it fascinating all the history here. My hometown is only as old as the 1900s."

"And it was run by mobsters." Kitty laughed."Viva Las Vegas, Sin City."

"And lucky us, we had to come to this god-forsaken country for a conference. At least the company is paying." Chas continued to type on his phone, the messages building up to be sent once cell service was available.

Annie rolled her eyes, having learned from the best, which Coyne caught in the rear-view mirror, and smiled.

"And Chas is the keynote speaker. He knows everything there is to know about Bitcoin." Annie smiled."Yet he finds history boring."

"Boring, boring, boring. If I've seen one rock, I've seen one hundred." Charles gripped his phone."Is there any movement with these damn animals?" Suddenly, the chant song for the Fighting Irish filled the car. Without a word, he opened the rear door and exited the car as a sudden burst of wind whipped his tie around his neck and he hung on with one hand his suit jacket while the other held the phone."A signal!! I have to take this call. I'll meet you at the castle."

"Sir, I can wait for you!" Coyne advised as Chas

gave a dismissive wave of his hand.

"Never mind him. He gets in these moods."Again, from the plane, she realized the smallest event could set him off. She'd been married to someone with the same traits. Annie lowered the window to wave at Chas, so involved in his phone call he didn't notice as Coyne maneuvered off the road and onto the field to bypass the sheep.

His voice carried in the wind."Ben, what have you got for me? SHIT!"

Sheep manure seeped into the soles of his Ferragamo's, onto the hem of his trousers. "I stepped in sheep shit. Quit laughing Ben or I'll fire you. You know what, you are fired." Chas toed his shoe off and attempted to wipe his foot on the grass. "Why the hell did they have to book a Bitcoin conference in bloody Ireland?"

"*Stop!*" Annie ordered Coyne as she reached around the suitcase and unzipped it, the rear door already half open by her frantic pushing.

"Mom, what are you doing?" Kitty cried out. "OMG, Mom, you are so embarrassing."

Annie hobbled out of the car and back to where Chas was, falling to his feet and peeling off his green tartan sock.

"Lean on me!" She frantically pulled it off and used the makeup wipes to remove the foul-smelling poo from his feet. Too small to completely cover the area, the fecal matter overflowed onto her hands, her nails now brown. Ignoring her discomfort, she began wiping down his shoes and sliding his feet into a pair of sandals she had optimistically packed in case they made it to a beach.

It was a reversed Cinderella as he wore the too-small sandals.

He nodded as he continued his conversation, ignoring Annie and her manure-covered hands. "Now, what were you saying? Hang on a second. You keep cutting out. Apparently, if I get to the top of this hill, I should have better cell reception." He continued around the sheep, petting one aggressively on its butt.

Storming up the hill, like a tornado in full force, he suddenly spun around and landed on his back, inches from a metal culvert.

Pushing herself to her feet, she rushed toward him, as did Finn, who left his sheep in the capable paws of the Australian Shepherd.

"What the hell just happened?" Chas asked, as he attempted to sit up, his phone spewed from his hand and now under the hoof of the straggling sheep.

"Are you okay?" Finn asked in an accent sounding more like he stepped off a ship in Boston Harbor than the outskirts of Ireland.

"I feel like I was hit by a Mack truck." He rubbed his forehead and blanched when it came away covered in blood. Panicking, he reached into his jacket, then sighed deeply when he pulled out a plastic-wrapped 4-leaf clover.

"Thought I had lost this." He returned it to his pocket and laid back down.

A beautiful butterfly, its paper-thin wings glittered in the sunlight as it landed on his shoulder before flying off.

"Was that a butterfly or am I losing my mind?" Chas asked, reaching to try and catch it, despite it now being out of range.

Kitty came toward them, the leash of Madison in her hands. "Wow, that was really something. I saw it happen." She picked up the twig, which lay to the side of Chas' head. "Imagine this little stick packing such a wallop."

Chapter 10

DRURIE: NOW

"Duncan, you idiot!!" I telepathically sent as I often did when we were in what I liked to call human range. We didn't want to give away all our secrets, but we are quite far advanced from you folks. How else do you think we survived for so long?

"Hush, both of you." Pixie motioned back to us. *"I know you're using your minds, but let's use your heads."*

I didn't want to tell her that didn't make sense. I mean, I did like her and eventually wanted to have those glossy wings wrapped around my torso, so I shut off my brain.

I crouched down closer to hide as she did a quick inventory of the injuries. With a gossamer touchdown on the man's jacket, Pixie rested for a minute, before skirting off into the western breeze.

"It was an accident," Duncan yelled into my elongated ear now that we were out of hearing range from the humans.

"According to Elmville, there are no such things as accidents." I strained my voice to be heard over the sound of an approaching wren that, like all wrens, had the attention span of a gnat and almost sideswiped us. If not for the alertness of Pixie, we would be in a worse fate than the human with the shillelagh indent on his noggin.

"What, so now you're quoting your brother?" Duncan asked, gripping his cap with both hands as I turned and stuck my tongue out at him.

With the strong tailwind, we flew past Dun Laoghaire, before turning northward, I saluted the 1847 lighthouse which brought many a ship into the harbor safely. The sharp breeze grew slightly colder as we began our descent into the grounds of Castle Whitestone.

Pixie crested her wings backward to create a downdraft as Duncan began his history lesson, which each of us leprechauns knew verbatim from the cradle, but he felt the need to recite.

"Built in the 10th century by the Normans, it was a medieval stronghold and has always been occupied. Originally a timber house, the keep was eventually replaced by stone. It has been in the same family since the 14th century and continues today to be owned by the Tobin family, where it is now a Taisce or the Irish equivalent to a National Trust and open to the public. Inside, there are underground servants' tunnels, rooms for the pruning of flowers, in addition to the observatory and eight-foot-high maze. A sunken bowling green, and water garden are surrounded by a forest where if you're quiet you will hear leprechauns laugh."

"Fiddle sticks. When have you ever heard a leprechaun laugh?" I asked Duncan as Pixie's anat skidded to a stop on a marble statue at the front of Castle Whitestone.

"Off you go. Give a holler if you need a pickup.

I'm headed out into the woods to meet up with Trixie. Tootles." Flipping her left wing at us, she flew off into the trees with nary a backward glance as we skittled down the sculpture, across the cobblestone drive, and rather than climbing the marble steps, we ventured into the shrubbery and our secret entrance. Tucked into the side of the grand entrance, hidden to the human eye, at first glance no more than a small pebble against a wooden trellis, but on closer examination, the jackstone was a door handle, the trellis the door itself.

An intricate series of tunnels wound through the walls, a peephole every three hundred feet in the most inconspicuous places. A bobbin of thread became a stool for us to stand on to see out into the main foyer. I climbed upon it as Duncan impatiently stomped his foot.

"Calm down, I just want to get the lay of the land," I ordered as I closed one eye to see better as I looked out onto the sign-in desk, through the eye of a peacock that graced the wallpaper.

I saw a river of sweat drip down onto the green Castle Whitestone golf shirt, as Flossy typed furiously on the keyboard. One of the major events I knew for a fact Flossy was not a fan of, was line-ups, telling me once she felt inadequate when people were made to wait. The slow internet connections through the old stone walls were not advantageous to speed up lines, thus the sweat. I whistled a high-pitched note linking into the server and the grin emanating from her face showed me it worked.

"Here are your keys for the two rooms."

She handed one to an older female while a younger girl almost saw me. I skittered out of sight as Flossy handed another to the man who had been hit because of Duncan's carelessness. "Peter will get your bags and I'll send up the doctor to have a look at your wound. It does look very nasty." Flossy waved over Peter and whispered her orders. "Once you get settled in your rooms, there is tea and crumpets set out in the room to the right of those stairs. Please help yourself." She handed the younger girl a fan of brochures. "We have several tours planned for those not directly involved with the convention. Sign-up is over by the podium and we just ask you to arrive fifteen minutes before the tour leaves."

I carefully climbed down off the bobbin, glad last time I was here I had secured it with a wad of gum and it was still stuck there. Elmville had a habit of retracing my steps and removing all the improvements I had implemented. Little devil he was.

I scampered to keep up with Duncan, who was waddling through the tunnel like he had a firecracker up his butt.

Breathless, I finally caught up to him, after ten minutes of seesawing betwixt and between the cracks in the mortar. It was exhausting, and I was not a young leprechaun. I was over seven hundred in human years, so when I say I've been there, done that, and purchased the t-shirt, you can believe me. Climbing down the keystones, I aligned myself beside him as we faced out the mouse hole discreetly hidden behind an Edwardian blue and white vase on a brass stand.

Suddenly, the bedroom door pushed open and the backdraft pulled us out of the hole and into the main room, right into the path of a large mobile rectangle headed right for the vase and us.

Chapter 11

KITTY: NOW

"Wow, Mom, this room is really something." I rushed into the room to grab the wayward suitcase as it streaked across the polished floor, which creaked with every step I took. "I thought the lobby was really something with all the wood paneling, and did you see the size of those portraits? They were larger than life-size. I can't imagine having to wear those dresses and the fancy hairstyles." I looked down at my attire and grinned. "We've sure come a long way." I flung myself down onto the double bed, running my fingers along the quilted bedspread. Embroidered with bees, butterflies, and hummingbirds, the reds and golds especially stood out against the green background. It was like I was lying in a field of wildflowers, so vivid the intricate work, I could almost hear the sounds. I gazed at the red velvet canopy drapes before turning my head toward the paneled wood on the ceiling of the canopy as well as the headboard. "Ben is redeeming himself. I always wanted to sleep in a canopy bed and best yet, I don't have to clean it. Can you imagine the time it would take dusting to get in all the crevices?"

"Your friend is something else," my mother answered absently as she opened her computer bag and settled into the workstation. Ben's Bible opened to the

Castle Whitestone page. My friend was a regular at the local craft store, and he'd outdone himself with pictures and glitter glue. "Shit!"

"Mom, what's the matter? Don't you think you should put something down on the desk? You don't want to scratch it. You're always on me to get a coaster so I don't mark the end table and it's not anywhere near as old as this one. Not to mention that Ben's glitter will be all over the place." I scootched to the end of the bed, and the room was suddenly quiet except for the scratching. "Mom, canopy or no canopy, if there's mice in this room, I'm not sleeping here." I stood on the bed, searching. "Mom, it sounds like it's coming from behind that vase. I'm not getting down to check."

"Kitty, it's an old house and I'm sure there might be critters in the wall, but I will have a look for you. It doesn't matter I have to put the finishing touches on this speech for Chas."

"Mom, you're not a babysitter to him. Wait! What? Why are you working on his speech? That's Ben's job and now we have cell service at the Castle, he can get ahold of Ben and have him do it." I paused to catch my breath. "He's a grown man and I'm sure he can write his own speech. Besides, what do you know about neurosurgery?"

The thought of mice was scaring me. There was nothing I hated more than mice. Some folks had snakes. I had mice.

"What did you say about neurosurgery?" My mom groaned as she lowered herself to her hands and knees and felt around behind the vase. "Kitty, there's nothing here. If there were, we would see mouse droppings and there's nothing. Now do you mind?" She pulled herself up and went back to the workstation. "I really have to get this accomplished. The sooner I do, then the sooner we can go exploring. Why don't you have a nap?"

"Mom, I'm not five years old. I don't need a nap and didn't you notice all the tables and flags set up by the dining room about neurosurgery?" I picked at my thumbnail watching my mother become more unhinged than normal and that was saying something.

"Shit! The conference we're supposed to attend was two days ago. With the frigging time change, we missed it. Oh damn, Ben really screwed up." She sank further down into the minutely padded chair, sobs resonating through the room.

"Mom, it will be okay. It was an honest mistake, and Chas will understand. It's Ben's problem, not ours. We can use the time to see the sights in the area." I gathered together the pamphlets Flossy at the front desk had handed us, flicking through them with nails Mom had treated me to as a thank you for bringing her along. I didn't tell her Ben insisted I bring her. He was such a mother's boy. He incorrectly assumed because he wanted to bring his mom, I would too. You think he would have listened to all my venting about my mom to have me bring someone else. I guess we really know who listens to whom.

"How am I going to tell him?"

Her sobbing was interrupted by a knock at the door as someone tried the door handle.

"Annie, it's me, Chas. Open the door!"

Chapter 12

ANNIE: NOW

"Oh, your head looks a lot better." She ushered him into the room and shot Kitty a look to let her know she would handle things. She had to get ahead of this situation before he blew his top.

"Yes, the doctor did a bang-up job, though I do feel like I'm wearing a turban. I don't believe there's any gauze left in Ireland." He rubbed the dressing.

"Maybe you should leave it alone," Kitty commented, watching from the bed. "Mom and I were going to go on a tour of the castle and it starts in ten minutes, every hour on the hour. So, Mom, we'd better get moving."

"Why don't you go downstairs and let them know I'll be along?" Annie grabbed her hand, pulled her off the bed, and pushed her out the door. "I'll be there shortly."

"That's okay, I'll wait for you." Kitty leaned against the door frame, picking at one of the lacquered nails.

"Is my speech finished?" Chas flopped into the antique embroidered chair and winced as his head hit the wood surrounding the frame. "The highlight of the trip is meeting Sir Alfred. He and I have a lot to discuss."

"Umm, there's something I need to tell you." Annie bit her lip and sat on the edge of the chair directly in front of Chas, the white stone fireplace providing a lovely backdrop under happier circumstances.

He held up his hand like a traffic cop, stunning her into silence. "Ben screwed up and you didn't catch it. I saw you on the plane reading through the folder like it was the latest bestselling novel and you didn't catch it. The one task you were given, to get me into the Bitcoin Convention you messed up. You're fired."

"Bu-but," Annie stammered, not wanting to glance at her daughter, her eyes welling with tears. "I don't work for you, so you can't fire me. We heard you fired Ben earlier today. You were yelling so loud, we could hear you as we pulled away."

"Can't you give her a chance to explain?" Kitty glared at him. "Have you never made a mistake? Ben doesn't deserve to be fired; he made an error."

Elvis singing "Viva Las Vegas" interrupted and Kitty glanced at her phone. "Look, it's Ben now."

She read the text and smiled. "Mom, it's okay. Ben quit this afternoon and starts work tomorrow for your favorite singer, Cacti. We're getting front row and backstage passes."

"You, young lady, should be seen and not heard. This has nothing to do with you. I had big plans to bring Chasworth Industries forward. The contacts I would have made at the conference would have been huge. Your friend, as well as your mother, due to their incompetence, have ruined any and all chances of that. I must head back to the States and figure out plan B." The veins in his neck stood out in ridges, like a road map.

"You're a real jerk," Kitty blurted out.

"You're correct, young lady." He administered a condescending tone. "I never make errors. I leave it to my staff, who obviously are paid way too much." He rose from the chair, his long strides taking him to the door in record time. "Enjoy the rest of your time here. Everything is paid for. It will be coming out of Ben's last paycheck."

Kitty slammed the door on his exit, and leaned against it, after sliding the deadbolt. Kitty ran into the bathroom and grabbed a roll of toilet paper, handing it to her mom. "We've got this."

"I know I wasn't working for him, but it was nice to feel wanted again, but his attitude reminded me so much of your father, that's what upset me the most."Annie blew her nose and the sound trumpeted through the room."Come on, we can sit here feeling sorry for ourselves or we can go and explore the Emerald Isle." Jumping out of the chair, she rushed toward the bed, picking up the brochures. "Let's do a tour of the castle first. Look at these, they are so outdated and the photo is blurred. Mom, I could do a better job blindfolded."

Annie flushed the tissue down the toilet and used a washcloth to clean up her face. Adding some of her own brand of lotions, moisturizer, and concealer, she rubbed and blended them into her skin before pushing back her shoulders, brushing her teeth, and exiting the bathroom.

"Come on, Kitty. What are you sitting around for? Let's do some exploring." Grabbing her daughter's hand, she blocked Chas on her phone, and grinned like a Cheshire cat. "He is going to be so helpless without me. He was like a child on the plane. Couldn't decide between the peanuts and the banana bread. I would have written a bang-up speech and frankly, Kitty, as the Irish say: If work was a bed, he'd be sleeping on the floor."

Chapter 13

COYNE: NOW

"Top of the morning to you two lovely ladies." Annie and Kitty walked to the reception desk where Coyne was chatting with Flossy. "Are you here to join my little tour?"

"Coyne, it's the afternoon." Annie gave him a small smile as he took in her red eyes and glanced over to her daughter, who shrugged her shoulders.

"Yes, I'm checking out." Chas' voice bellowed across the lobby. Flossy cast a quick look in Coyne's direction as her fingers flew across the computer keys.

"I'm sorry you didn't enjoy your stay."

"I would have if my incompetent colleague didn't book the wrong flights so we missed the Bitcoin conference and I have no use for neurosurgery."

"He'd have to have a brain to attend," Coyne stage whispered to Annie and Kitty.

"Yes, it is confusing with dates," Flossy attempted to calm him down. "I'll put the credit on the card the room was originally charged to and you'll be good to go."

Grabbing his luggage by the handle, it jerked and spun around, the third wheel spinning in a different direction. Yanking it like a disobedient animal, the scowl on his face said it all. He reached into his pocket and pulled out his 4-leaf clover. "This is supposed to bring me luck. Well, the hell with it." He tossed it in the trash receptacle by Flossy. "Would it be too much to ask to have a taxi drive me to the airport?"

"I'll call someone now."

"What about that guy? He drove me here." Chas pointed toward Coyne, who immediately turned his back.

"Sorry, sir. He's hosting a tour, but his father should be available."

"Where's the bloke I have to drive?" Just inside the entrance doors, an elderly man leaned heavily on a cane, puffing on a stubby cigar. The smoke billowed around him in a perfect smoke ring. His gray hair spiked in every direction, and from his tartan vest, he pulled out a pocket watch.

"Dad, he's right there." Coyne pointed out Chas as he turned toward the women. "Don't worry, he's in good hands. Now, let's begin our tour, shall we?"

"Come on then," Coyne's father ordered. "I haven't got all day to get you to the airport."

He turned to walk outside as Chas yelled, "What about my luggage?"

Coyne's father turned and gave Chas the once over. "You've got two good legs so use them. There's a dart tourney tonight at the Leprechaun's Door, and I have to get a good seat. Bye, Flossy, and thanks for the call."

"My dad doesn't have much patience for idiots," Coyne said with a wink. "Now, for our tour."

Chapter 14

DRURIE: NOW

"I gave you a bit of the history of the castle in the car ride here, but if you follow me, this is the Grand Room." Coyne and the two women entered the room. The walls were covered with tapestries of knights and fair maidens. Green velvet loveseats were set in threesomes, surrounding a natural stone fireplace, the crackling blaze warming the room. "This was the social room of the castle. If you join me over here by this wall covering, it's my favorite." He waved them over and stood back with his arms behind him. It was a tapestry of a majestic lion, a knight, his helmet in his other hand feeding it grass as a maiden sat on a plaid blanket gazing at the knight.

"Wow, is that you?" Annie asked as she studied the knight and Coyne.

"Here he goes again, showing the guests this tapestry," Drurie telepathed to Duncan as they watched the events unfold. *"You can set your pocket watch by him."*

"It's my father's great-grandfather, but that wasn't what I wanted you to see."

Drurie elbowed his friend. "Shh, this is the good part."

"If you can tear yourself away from my handsome

relative, tell me what you see in the folds of the maiden's dress."

Annie and Kitty stood closer to the wall hanging and Kitty yelled out. "I see it, do you see it, Mom? It's right there." Kitty stretched out her hand, then thought better of it. "Sorry, I guess I'm not supposed to touch it."

"Good, you found it," Coyne said as Annie muttered. "My eyes aren't as good as yours. What am I missing?"

"Mom, right in the corner there, in the shading of her dress, you can see a leprechaun poking its head out."

With Kitty pointing to the obvious, Annie grinned. "I see it now."

Drurie punched his arm in the air. *"Got it in one. Remember the time Coyne had to basically draw a road map for the tour and the one who was drunk and almost spilled her red wine. Coyne almost had a coronary."*

"Leprechauns, they even had them back then?" Annie asked, surveying the rest of the room as her eyes settled on the dollhouse.

"Wait until I give you a tour of Newgrange, if you're interested? There's an interesting leprechaun drawing on the wall."

"We'd love to. It's not like we're doing anything else before we leave, but what is this?" Annie walked over to the dollhouse, peering down into the windows.

"This is an exact replica of Castle Whitestone. If you view it from this side, you can see the inside."

"Look, Mom, there's our room. It's complete even with the vase beside the fireplace." Annie and Kitty leaned into the house, Kitty excitedly pointing out the various items.

"This was created by my grandfather. He was a major woodworker and made it for my mom when she was ten. As you can see, the rooms haven't been changed since." In the miniature Grand Room, the details were precise down to the wall hangings and a miniature doll house.

"Is the miniature dollhouse detailed?"

Coyne laughed. "No, that's where the Leprechauns live."

"Great. Why does he always have to bring us into the conversation?" Drurie telepathically messaged Duncan.

"Cause when he mentions us, it ups his street cred, and the girls like it," Duncan commented, scratching his nose.

"I could spend all day looking at the miniature furnishings." Annie smiled. "My grandfather used to like the miniature train tracks, and he had it all set up in his basement. I always felt like Gulliver."

"Okay, let's head back to the lobby and we'll go downstairs to the tunnels, the wine cellar, and the cells."

"Wait, there're cells here?" Kitty asked, anxiously looking at her mom.

"Cells were in every castle, to house the invaders they didn't kill, but there aren't any ghosts. The leprechauns took care of that."

"Mom, are you okay if I go back to the room and lie down?" Kitty asked as Coyne held his breath waiting for Annie's reply. He liked the American lass and wanted to spend time with her alone. "You go on with Coyne and I'll be fine."

"What about the mice?" Annie asked.
"I'll be fine."

Chapter 15

ANNIE: NOW

"Why were you asking about mice?" Coyne asked, opening the door at the far end of the lobby and allowing Annie to enter first.

"Kitty thought she heard rustling behind the vase in our bedroom, but I looked and didn't see anything there." Side by side, they walked along the arched stone walkway, water dripping softly along the walls.

"Probably just the leprechauns checking out the occupants of the room." He chuckled. "Don't worry. They won't hurt you. Well, Elmville might, but they seem to keep him in check."

"Wait, you know the names of the leprechauns?" Annie stopped and grabbed his arm, ignoring the spark ignited from the touch.

"Any Irishman worth his weight knows the names of the locals." He took her hand. "The tunnel gets a little slippery here, and I don't want you to hurt yourself." His hand had the coarseness of a man who wasn't afraid of manual labor and she held on to it like it was the last life preserver on the Titanic.

"These tunnels were originally constructed by the Romans. Ireland is like lasagna, layers upon layers of stone."

"Imagine the history down here." Annie stopped

and looked in awe at the torches lighting their way, the flickering flames casting a glow onto his face, his eyes lighting like a firefly.

"These tunnels used to be a flurry of activity with kitchen staff running to and up the stairs to the dining room, up to the bedrooms with bed warmers. They must have been pretty fit," Coyne lectured, not letting go of her hand. "If you look over here, you'll actually see Roman carvings." Standing behind her, he reached around her, and pointing with his other hand, he traced the markings on the stone to bring it to her attention.

Annie turned her head, his lips so close to her cheek, the atmosphere so intimate with the torches, the seeping water on the stones creating a mini waterfall. She inhaled his scent of forest leaves, and wood smoke, an earthy aftershave.

He turned her slightly and dropped his mouth onto hers, a butterfly kiss. Not demanding, but encouragement of adventures forthcoming.

"Sorry, I shouldn't have done that." Coyne stepped back and dropped her hand like it was as hot as the torch.

"No need to apologize, but I really should get back to Kitty."

"Sure, of course." Traveling back the way they had come, passing wooden vaulted doors, the largest with a massive metal lock.

"What's behind the door?" Annie asked, as her shoe slipped on the moist floor. Coyne grabbed her, keeping her upright. "Why is it locked?"

Chapter 16

1800s: KINGSTOWN, IRELAND

The deck of the merchant ship Magna, her sails lowered now they were in dock, was lined with foreign sailors gazing in awe at the landscape of Ireland. Having been at sea for fourteen weeks, they longed to walk on land but knew they had to first unload the cargo.

Sacks of potatoes heaved from one sailor to the next until they reached the top of the ship, where they were unceremoniously dumped onto the dock.

Elmville listened to the foreign language, understanding a bit of the lingo, not knowing where they were going to find chunky Irish women looking for exotic lads, and chuckled as he got busy with the task at hand.

Farmers lined up along the pier, handing the captain coins for a sack. Depending on how affluent the farmer determined how many sacks he received.

Elmville hopped up and onto the wooden cart, already filled with five of the bags, the horses snorting and grunting in protest with the weight. He used his shillelagh to poke a hole in the burlap and tossed in a handful of phytophthora infestans water mold from the side of the ship. He repeated it with each of the bags, continuing to whistle, the horses and their keen hearing, the only ones to hear.

Days later, Elmville crawled into the ear of the lead horse, a warm cozy abode as it pulled the wooden plow along the field, creating rows to which Donal planted the lumper potato.

Not content to only infect the potatoes in the sacks he had infected with the contaminated spores, Elmville waited with extreme patience. He crawled out of the horse's ear, his home causing him dizziness as the beast of burden found an annoyance in his ear and kept shaking his head backward and forward.

Elmville held in his breath and released it in one go, the spores from the infected plants now contaminating all the other plants as well. Elmville was the root cause of the Potato Famine, the devastation, the loss of lives—it was on him. Yet, he wasn't going to take the blame or the credit, he would let that fall onto his brother. Drurie would be blamed, Elmville would frame his kin. What brother didn't want to get off scot-free when his sibling could take the fall? The old potato spore in the vest pocket would seal his fate.

Several years later, dust blew across the barren fields as the farmer caught a whiff of the decaying livestock, stomachs engorged lying in the middle of the potato fields. Donal Tobin leaned on his pitchfork, wiped the sweat from his brow, and cried. His farm was considered Ground Zero, his crops and livestock the most destroyed by what the newspapers were calling the Gorta Mor. Adjacent farmland became infected as the spores from the fungus became airborne, settling on each of the host plants.

He was an outcast, ostracized by his friends, his family. The blame didn't fall on the country who sent them the tubers. Even then the politicians knew they had to remain friends, so the accusations fell onto Donal Tobin and his family. Neighbors were leaving for the United States and Canada by the shipload, not stopping to bid farewell, but instead spitting on him as they walked toward the harbor. Lads he had known since he was kneehigh to a grasshopper, now turned their back on him when they crossed paths.

Even his wife Edith, his sun and his moon, would be ignored by townsfolk when she tried to make conversation. Donal could brave it for himself, but when it came to being rude to Edith, he could take no more.

With his shoulders back, he walked toward his mud cabin as smoke rose through the door. Donal had soused out the best location, one on top of a high grade, the view of the harbor breathtaking. He had completed his due diligence with the fairies. He had marked each of the corners of his intended new cabin with a large rock and placed a smaller one on top. Leaving it overnight, he was relieved to see the smaller stones hadn't been disturbed. This meant planning approval had been given by the fairies and leprechauns. His neighbor had come back to his own section the next day to find the stones had been tossed to the sides. When he found another area and did the same, all was good.

Granite stones were used in the walls, with trimmed sod filling in the seams. He'd learned to support each of the walls with timber beams, and in one particularly bad spot on the roof. Each sandstone rock in the fireplace he had painstakingly laid out in a pattern, so it would be perfect for his bride, the love of his life, Edith. The roof he had thatched and harvested from crops in the fields, fields now barren with rotting crops. While others were leaving without a backward glance, months ago when he had suggested they do the same, Edith had tucked her tiny hand in his, her Galway shawl wrapped around her shoulders, protection against the cold northern wind, and shook her head.

Lowering his head so he didn't crack it on the door frame, the one concession he forgot to measure when he was building the cottage. He expected to see Edith sitting in her favorite chair, to the left side of the fireplace, her Galway shawl, fraying at the corners from the amount of use, was draped over her lap. Smoke rose from the fireplace, escaping through holes, but the room was still smoky, cloudy, foggy.

Donal's breeches hung on him. The pride Edith took in the whiteness of Donal's shirt now passed, as a cough racked through her.

"Wife, you shouldn't sit so near the fire. The fumes will not be good for you." Donal stood beside her and rested his hand on her once vibrant red curls. Now, along with the food in their bellies, the luster and sheen of her hair were no more.

"Do you bring any news?" Edith asked, grasping his hand, her cough raking through her bones.

"No, there was a steady stream of people leaving today. Are you sure, wife, you do not want to join them? I can afford to send you over to the New World, and I can join you once I get things secure here." He knelt beside her chair. "Wife, we can begin again."

"If you so want to go, we can, Husband, but I will not go without you. I will wait for you to secure things and we shall go together, the four of us."

Edith took his hand and placed it on her belly.

"Husband, it is not a good time for me to travel as I am with child."

"We will have another child to carry on the name and all this land will be his. God willing, it will be a boy. Surely this plague cannot go on forever." He stood up to stoke the fire, as his daughter moved from the shadows, a corn husk doll clutched tightly in her hands. "Susan, it will be up to you to assist your mother."

"Husband, I was afraid to tell you as it will be another mouth to feed and we cannot fill the stomachs of the ones we have."

"We will be fine." Donal kissed the top of her head and gathered Susan in his arms and spoke to her doll. "At least this is one mouth I do not have to find food for."

Susan lisped seriously. "Father, she must eat as well."

He put his daughter down on her mother's lap. "Come hell or high water, we will survive."

Chapter 17

KITTY: NOW

"Mom, how was the tour? Did I miss anything?" Mom came into the bedroom, her face the color of a cardinal. "Why is your face so red? Was the tour so exhausting? Lots of steps? Do you need to lie down?" I moved over to make room for her on the bed.

"Umm, no, I'm okay, but I think I will have a lie-down. The last couple of days have been stressful, and I feel like I could drop dead on my feet." Mom crawled onto the bed and I tucked the quilt around her.

"Really, thanks for the sweatshirt. I really appreciate it, even if I don't always show it." I reached out and grabbed her hand, lacing my fingers with hers. My elegant nails were a sharp contrast to her short dirty ones, but I wouldn't want it any other way. She was my mom and she didn't need to work for such a creep, especially when it wasn't her job.

"Kitty, thank you." Mom pressed her hand tighter to mine. "I know I haven't always been a great mom, but I've tried." She wiped a tear away with the other hand.

"Mom, don't cry." I snuggled in closer and laid my head on her shoulder as she wrapped her arm around me.

"Sorry to get so emotional." Mom sniffed and

shook her head as if ridding herself of the negativity. "I've tried so hard since your dad left and sometimes it just feels like nothing goes right." She sniffed again. "When I think I might have lost you the night of the accident, I just couldn't bear it." Mom grabbed a tissue from up her sleeve like Houdini and wiped her nose. "Why were you out there to begin with?"

"Mom, can we drop it? It didn't work out, anyway." I jerked up from the bed and went and sat in the chair by the fireplace. "Way to ruin the mood."

I knew I was being prickly, but sometimes my mom and I were like chalk and cheese. She just didn't get it.

"All I did was ask why you were out on a road, a road without streetlights in the middle of nowhere, and then to come up with the cockamamie answer that you almost hit a little green man. The only answer I can come up with was you were high."

"Geez, Mom, I wasn't high or drunk or anything." I went into the bathroom, slamming the door. Turning on the tap, I tried to drown her out. I could still hear her talking.

Nothing calmed me down like a hot shower, so I threw my clothes on the floor and adjusted the taps so it was hot. Beside the rainforest nozzle was a wall container filled with shampoo, conditioner, and body wash. Cautiously, I poured some of the body wash into my hand and inhaled. Ambushed with the scents of lilacs, roses, and rosemary, I quickly washed it off and used mom's lotions to remove the overwhelming fragrance.

I stepped out of the bathtub and grabbed one of the hotel embroidered towels, sinking into the fluffiness of

71

the extra-long fibers. This was not my home bath towel decorated with a hot air balloon and the Vegas sign, so threadbare it was see-through. And this one was big. I could almost fit another person in it with me. If there was such a person I would want to share with. And no, I don't know why Finn the shepherd popped into my head.

Mom was on the phone when I stepped out of the bathroom, my fingers a makeshift comb through my hair.

"Sure, we'll meet you there. It's not like we're doing anything else." Mom giggled. Wait, Mom giggled. My mom does not giggle. My mom does not do anything fun. As Finn says *minus crais*. Okay, he meant me, not her, but what had the leprechauns done with my mom?

"That was Coyne. He wants us to meet him at the front desk after we've finished dinner. He's going to escort us, that was his wording, escort us, to the Leprechaun's Door." Mom headed to her suitcase and began tossing her clothes. "Why didn't I bring anything to wear to a pub?"

"Maybe 'cause you figured you'd be working the whole time for jerkface and picking up sheep shit off his shoes. Oh wait, that already happened." I was a bitch, but I couldn't help it.

"Kitty, you're not helping matters. What are you going to wear?" Mom asked as she held up a red lace bra and quickly shoved it back into the netting of her suitcase.

"I'm not going. I'm going to spend the night in with a book." Hot corporate, suit-wearing guys were my idea of a good time.

"Oh right, Coyne said Finn said you wouldn't want to go and show how Vegas chicks didn't know their arse from their elbows." Mom held out a white wool sweater and jeans. "I think this will do. I hope I'll be warm enough. Maybe tomorrow I can do some shopping and treat myself. Nothing expensive, mind you, just a little something."

"Wait, Finn said what about me?" What was this guy's problem? I flopped down in the chair only to stand up and start going through my own suitcase. This was a high-class towel, it didn't even fall with all my vigorous activities.

"He told Coyne you didn't know your arse from your elbow." Mom rooted her makeup bag out of the suitcase and headed into the bathroom. "Are you okay with having dinner with me beforehand? If not, I can grab something at the pub, though Flossy said the fish and chips tonight were to die for."

"I'll show him "Vegas chicks" (I was not above making air quotes) do know our arse from our elbows. My degree will come in handy when I wipe the floor with him." I slid on a pair of underwear, my favorite jeans and my new Harvard sweatshirt. I know you know Mom bought it and I didn't actually go there, but the online college I attended didn't have sweatshirts, though they did send me some really cool pens, the kind with the floaties. I can't count the number of times I played with the pen while trying to write an essay on Life Coaching. I am an official Life Coach. I have the certificate and all to prove it, even if it was an online course. It came with a very impressive gold seal.

I joined Mom in the bathroom, standing side by side as we did our makeup, avoiding her eyes in the mirror.

"So, will you join me for dinner?" Mom asked, putting on mascara. I have never seen my mom with mascara, but there you go.

"Sure." My phone buzzed with an incoming text. I grabbed a jacket and tied up my running shoes as I read the text.

"Is it good news?" Mom asked, leaving the bathroom, tossing her makeup bag into her suitcase, and grabbed her own jacket, tucking her phone into an inside pocket.

"Yeah, sure. I got a call back for Walking With Woofers."

"That's great, sweetheart. It will be good exercise, and think of all the fresh air." Mom ran back into the bathroom, and I could see her pursing her lips, evening out her lipstick.

"Well, we'll see. I mean, having a call back to walk dogs isn't really brain surgery."

"No, brain surgery is the conference downstairs." She laughed. "Come on, let's have dinner."

We headed down the central red-carpeted stairs, following the queue of gray-haired couples into the dining room. Observing the Seat Yourself sign, Mom immediately headed over to the window where we had an unobstructed view of the flowers, the purple lilacs in full bloom anchoring a water fountain, water spewing from a fish mouth. Short boxwoods intermixed with red and purple fuchsia formed a low maze where children were playing tag.

"Hard to believe you were that young once." Mom said, picking up the menu.

"What can I get you?" Flossy asked, filling our

water glasses before pulling papers from her apron pocket.

"You suggested the fish and chips earlier, so I'll go with that. How about you, Kitty?"

"I'll have the same."

"You guys are easy. Can I interest you in a Guinness or how about a Leprechaun Coin?" Flossy asked, tucking her notepad back into her pocket.

"I think I'll pass. We're meeting up with Coyne and Finn after dinner to join in the Trivia Night, so we'd better keep our wits about us."

"Be careful of those two. They have been known to cheat." Flossy laughed as she headed into the kitchen to place their orders.

"Great, a couple of Irishmen who cheat, just what we need."

"Well, at least if we lose, we can blame it on them taking advantage." Mom laughed as she sipped her water.

I don't know what was in the water, but Mom was giggling and laughing an awful lot since Chas left, which I can only see as a good thing.

Mom and I watched the kids in the garden. I could smell the fish and chips, the salt and vinegar arousing my nose. My stomach rumbled as Flossy set the plates down in front of us and I grabbed one of the chips with my fingers, burning them in the process. Blowing on it, I ate it, savoring the salt and the light oil.

I added a mountain of ketchup, as well as trailing ketchup over the fries and fish, barely avoiding the coleslaw.

"Do you want some chips with your ketchup?" Coyne asked as he came by our table. "I've never seen anyone add so much ketchup to their chips."

"She's been like that forever," Mom said, flipping her hair back over her shoulder. "You should see her with mac and cheese, it was like a blood bath." She ran on. "I used to think it had something to do with my cooking, but I checked with her doctor and no, it was just something she liked to do. So like any good mother, I picked my battles and let her have all she wanted."

"TMI," I muttered, my head down, concentrating on my food, which, by the way, I would give five stars. Flossy was right. It was good.

"Well, you might want to have the sticky pudding as well, but hold off on the ketchup. You'll need the extra sugar high if you want to beat Finn tonight in Trivia. He's been practicing."

"I heard from a reliable source you guys like to cheat." I sipped my water, washing down the mouthful of fish.

"I bet you heard that lie from Flossy. She is a sore loser and refuses to play with us, thus the reason she's working the restaurant tonight." Coyne straightened up the salt and pepper shakers on the table as Flossy walked by with steaming plates of food. "Isn't that right, Flossy?"

"Yes, I'd rather make money than lose it by having to buy pints for you lot. Also, I promised Finn I would have a look in at the barn and keep an eye on Heldy."

Coyne glanced down at his watch. "We'll need to get a move on. Will you be ready in about ten minutes?"

I nodded when Mom glanced over at me. "Sounds good. We'll finish up here, use the washroom, and meet you in the lobby."

****

Finn and I trailed behind Mom and Coyne. Mom's chuckles could be heard back to Castle Whitestone, I'm sure.

"Your mom's ankle seems to be doing better. Coyne said she had a bit of a mishap at the airport," Finn mentioned as he picked up a stick and tore the bark off it as we walked.

"Yeah, she slipped on the flooring, but she wrapped it in a thick sock, and it seems to be doing the trick. Either that or Coyne is taking her mind off of the pain."

"He does have a way with the ladies. He has kissed the Blarney stone a few times." He ran his stick along a stone fence.

"You Irish have a lot of Blarney from what I've heard." I stopped to pick up a stone, the yellow colors glowing in the moonlight.

"Look, there's the Northern Cross." Finn pointed at the constellation. "And there's Aries."

"I'm an Aries. Did you do that on purpose?" I asked, glancing over at him. I must say he does clean up pretty good. One would never know he herds sheep by day. I got a whiff of his shampoo and it was *sooo* much better than the stuff in my shower. He smelled like grass and springtime.

"Yes, lass, I arranged the stars just for you. You'll have to wait around and see what I do for an encore. Yankee you will be duly impressed."

"Yankees are from the north and I'm from the south." Geez, did no one know our history?

"I'm not about to argue with someone who went to

Harvard." Finn bowed as he walked. "My apologies, lass."

We strolled through the village, the joined houses flush with the cobblestone sidewalk. I tried to avoid looking through the windows, but I couldn't help it. Talk about a microcosm of the Irish way of life. Every house we passed, well, those who had their drapes open to be fair, had some sort of dinner on their knees in front of the television. Some with the sound so loud I could make out the shows. It was actually quite comical as each television or telly, as they called it, was set to the same channel.

"Does everyone watch the same show?" I asked Finn as we walked past.

"Have you never seen Coronation Street? It's British but I saw it played in Canada when I was there."

"Wait, when were you in Canada?" I stopped and pulled at his shirt.

"My nan lives there with my uncle, so I try to get over every couple of years and she comes here as often as she can."

"That is soooo unfair," I admitted as we passed a charity shop and a corner store.

"What? You're upset because these stores are closed. They open at nine a.m. and you can visit them then. Tell them Finn sent you and they won't shut the door on your face."

"No, I'm upset because you will know Canada trivia and have an unfair advantage. Flossy said you were a cheater."

"It's hardly cheating because I listen to my grandmother and sit beside her while she watches the Canadian news. Miss Harvard."

Mom turned around and pointed at the charity shop. "Kitty, let's go and visit there tomorrow."

Music with the emphasis on fiddles, bellowed out of the open door as we approached the Leprechaun's Door. Housed in a stone cottage, the thatched roof hanging down almost to the stained-glass windows. Six tables sat outside the door; umbrellas advertising Guinness beer waved in the slight breeze.

Coyne held the door open and ushered us inside. Clouds of cigarette smoke created a fog-like atmosphere, the music almost silenced by the cheers at the dart board. Coyne's father clapped another man on the back, who tipped his flat cap Gatsby.

"Coyne, my boy, you're just in time. Art here isn't as good at darts as he thinks he is and bet me a Guinness he could reach zero before me. Well, the luck of the Irish wasn't on his side tonight. So, I'm off to the bar." He grinned and headed toward the bar waving a 5-pound note like it was the Irish flag. "Oh, what a fine pair of lasses you brought with you tonight, me boy. Diaduit. You two certainly make this pub a lot prettier. Tonight might be lucky for us all."

"Has your father been kissing the stone as well?" Mom asked Coyne.

"Dear, you have no idea." Coyne's father laughed as he wrapped an arm around Annie and led her toward the bar.

Chapter 18

ANNIE: NOW

"Coyne, I left me jacket on the chair over there, saving the table for you lot." He pointed, his arm wrapped around Annie, a lit cigarette almost burning a patron. "Since my son doesn't think I'm important enough, allow me to introduce myself and I'll show drinks for you lot." He stubbed his cigarette out in an overflowing ashtray on the bar and snapped his fingers."Erin, five beers for Coyne and his friends. And another for Art, but only fill it half full as he'll be crying in it. Though you'd think he'd be used to losing to me by now."

"Certainly, Sir Alfred." Erin wiped off the dark walnut bar with a towel she kept over her shoulder. Bottles of various shapes and sizes lined the wall behind the counter as beers on tap stood like toy soldiers, each with a unique handle advertising their wares. Annie checked them out, amazed at the imagination as one housed a cross, another a leprechaun, and still another a small door.

"The Leprechaun's Door has been around since the 1800s. If these walls could only talk. They have been privy to conversations about the potato famine, the great wars and heavens knows what else."Annie grabbed two of the beers, and Sir Alfred grasping the rest.

Smiling at the other patrons as she weaved her way to the table, Annie placed the drinks on the table, slopping some of the beer onto the coasters. Sir Alfred, when he eventually reached the table, put his three down, never spilling a drop before unceremoniously dropping five bags of potato chips on the table. "Lass, that's the waste of a good ale."

The crowd cheered, fists pumped in the air, eyes glued to the large screen television behind the bar. Sir Alfred spoke to Annie, his words were drowned out by the ruckus, but she nodded in agreement.

"It's been a long time since I was a waitress." Annie grinned, sliding into the seat beside Coyne.

"Mom, I didn't know you were a waitress," Kitty said, wiping off a beer foam mustache. "When was this?"

"I'm sure they don't want to hear about my adventures. Now, what's up with this Trivia?"

"Mom, do you notice the tables near us go silent when we speak?" Kitty asked, as indeed the nearby customers leaned toward the table, trying to appear they weren't listening in.

"That's because of your accents," Finn said, then took a sip of his beer. "We're used to our own, but foreigners are a rarity."

"You're a foreigner," Coyne said, poking his friend in the shoulder. "Oh, should I say an Irish wannabe?"

"Wait, you're a shepherd. Are you telling me you're not Irish, not a shepherd?" Kitty asked, pulling open a bag of onion and cheddar-flavored crisps. Passing her open bag around the table, she fished a couple out of the bag, scrunched her face when the flavor hit her tongue, and pushed the bag to the middle of the table. "Yuck, how can you guys like these?"

"They are an acquired taste, like Marmite," Finn said, grabbing a handful and washing them down with a gulp of beer.

"It even sounds disgusting," Kitty said. "What should we call our team? We are all playing on the same team, correct?"

"I think we'd better. You need our help, Harvard," Finn teased as he played with his coaster."How about the Harvard 5?"

"Or Smarty Pints?" Kitty grinned.

"Oh, I'm glad this young bird is on our team." Sir Alfred raised his glass in a toast. "Here's to the various countries winning tonight. Speaking of that, I'd better get us another round before Erin gets caught up in the Trivia and forgets how to pull a pint."

"Here, let me." Annie pulled some pound notes out of her jeans and pushed them into Sir Alfred's hand. "Don't want it to be said Americans don't pull their own weight."

Sir Alfred pushed back his chair and headed toward the bar, stopping at each table like he was a celebrity. His snow-white hair stood at attention despite his attempts at smoothing it.

"Your dad knows a lot of people but I guess it is a small town," Annie yelled into Coyne's ear. The music seemed louder than ever before.

"He got lucky with some investments and rather than keep it to himself, he shared and invested in the small businesses in town. He paid their rents for a year, and erected a bandstand in the town center. If you'd like, I can take you and Kitty on a tour tomorrow of

Dun Laoghaire."

"It sounds wonderful. I'll have to check with Kitty to make sure she doesn't have other plans, but I'd love to go." She squeezed his arm.

"Don't you be getting too frisky with my lad there," Sir Alfred said, setting all the beers on the table.

"You mean you could have carried them all by yourself, that I didn't need to help?" Annie gathered up the empty glasses and prepared to carry them back to the bar.

"Yes, but I would never say no to a lass helping to lighten my load."

Chapter 19

KITTY: NOW

Erin rang the brass bell hanging beside the bar. The music turned off mid-song, the pub now as silent as a funeral home.

"Lads and ladies, are your pencils sharpened?"

"Erin, I don't have a pencil!" A thick Irish accent yelled from the back corner, sounding like the singer Jonob had stepped into the pub.

"Paul David, of course you don't have a pencil. Come on up and grab one and get another iced water and note paper as well."

"Is that really Jonob?" I asked, craning my neck to see if it was him.

Avoiding my question, he doodled on the notepad. "If he is in town, he does like to stop in. He has a cottage in the area."

"That is so cool. Mom, did you hear Jonob is in the corner back there?"

"I would have thought going to Harvard and living in Las Vegas you would have seen lots of celebrities," Finn suggested, checking his phone before turning it back over.

"I saw a couple of Vegas headliners walking the Strip, but that's the extent of my celebrity sightings. But my friend Ben is going to be working for the famous singer, Cacti, who I adore, so hopefully, I'll get to meet her."

"She's so famous, we've even heard of her over here," Finn continued doodling, a sheep taking form.

"Okay, now we have Paul David or as your new friends call him, Jonob situated, does anyone else need anything before we get started? Yes, I know you will get thirsty, so during the contest, one at your table can come up and get a round. Remember, I said one. Okay, let the games begin, and remember folks, this is all for fun and charity."

"Charity?" Annie grabbed more bills from her pocket. "I didn't realize I needed to pay for Kitty and myself."

"All taken care of. All taken care of. Now let's just see how intelligent you Americans really are," Coyne said as Sir Alfred glanced at his son.

Chapter 20

1800s: KINGSTOWN, IRELAND

Warm sunlight streamed through the dusty windows of the cabin, rousing Donal from sleep. Dressed in his breeches, he rose from the straw mat on the floor and stoked the fire in the fireplace. He had constructed it in the middle of the room, to provide heat to all corners of the space, and away from the walls that might catch a wayward spark.

William and Susan stretched, the sunlight cast across their faces as they snuggled closer to their mother in the bed.

"Edith, go back to sleep. As we discussed, I'm going to take the horse and cart. I'll return as soon as I can, God willing."

"Husband, take William with you. He will be good company. It will be a good learning experience for him." She roused her son. "William, go with your father."

"Mama, I want to stay with you. It is so warm." William nuzzled closer to his mother.

"Your bones will turn to lard if you don't use them. Now get up, you lazy bones, and help your father." Edith threw the covers off her son. Susan didn't stir, playing possum as she opened one eye furthest away from her mother.

"It's so not right, Mother. Why do I have to get up out of this warmth, whereas Susan can stay here with you." William whined as Susan stuck her tongue out at him. "Mother, did you see what she did to me? Mother, will you punish her?" William stood upright, towering over his mother and sister in the bed.

"William, come along," Donal commanded. "Leave your sister alone. She is but a girl and one day she will marry off and become someone else's problem. You are the man; all this will be yours." Donal made a sweeping gesture.

William waved his fist at Susan, who smiled and wrapped her arm around her mother as William followed his father out of the sod cabin.

"Where are we going, Father? Why do we need to take the horse?" William held onto the reins as his father lifted the saddle onto the horse's back.

"Have you never heard curiosity killed the cat, my son?" Tightening the straps under the animal, he attached the cart as well.

"Father, why the saddle and the cart?" William asked.

"The saddle is worth a lot of money, and we will need everything in our negotiations."

Edith and Susan came to the door of the sod cabin, Edith tucking a towel around her famous cornbread. The thought of the warm bread caused William's stomach to rumble. She placed another towel into the back of the cart, before patting her husband on his arm.

"Be successful, dear husband. You have the Blarney on your side."

With a wave, Father led the horse as they walked along the lazy beds in the fields, the rotting leaves soaked through with the recent rain. A lone hawk circled overhead, ever on the alert.

They walked past sod cabins, all abandoned, doors left ajar.

"Father, what happens to all this land now the tenants have left?"

"I have a meeting set up for that very reason. You are a smart young boy. I will be meeting with the landlords who own the acreage adjoining our fields. I hope they will sell me the vacant land at a fair price." Donal led the horse along the gravel road, the clip-clop from the horse and the cranking of the cart's wheels musically adding to their trip.

William walked alongside the cart. He was grown up enough to know while his father walked, he walked as well. His eye caught a shiny stone, and when he bent to pick it up, he realized it was a silver locket.

"Father, look what I found for us." William held out his palm.

"Good find, my son." Donal wiped the locket on his dusty pants. "But it is yours to keep. Tuck it away someplace safe."

"Father, you said these lands will be mine one day, so I would like to help you." William tried to push the necklace back into his father's hand.

"Son, I do not need your help, though I do appreciate it." He glanced up at the sky, suddenly dark. "How about we stop under that elm tree and have some of the wonderful bread your mother baked for us?" The words weren't out of his mouth before the skies opened up and the rain teemed down.

Side by side, they sat in the back of the cart, Donal pulling off a huge chunk of the bread for each of them, before wrapping what remained back in the towel. "I was a lucky sod when your mother agreed to marry me."

"She is a good mother," William agreed as he swallowed a bit of the bread, then held his hands into a cup shape so he could gather some of the rainwater.

"That she is, dear boy. I could not ask for a better wife. Do you know I asked her if she wanted to leave many years ago when the famine was at its worse? Her answer was she was with child, that child being you, and she would stay. I told her I would send her and you as well as Susan and come later when I had more money saved. Yet, she wanted to wait until we could all travel together. She does believe in family."

Chapter 21

KITTY: NOW

Noise in the pub increased with the amount of beers poured. Kitty was in charge of writing down the answers, and if Finn told her one more time she spelled flavor wrong, she would throttle him.

"Okay, everyone ready? Here's the last question of the night." Erin rang the bell to silence the room. "Is everyone ready? It's an easy one. What do the hundred folds in a chef's hat represent?" She smiled, tipping over the salt timer.

"Come on, Harvard, you've got this." Finn turned his phone back over and checked the screen.

"Finn, there's no checking your phone," Erin called from across the room.

"Sorry, I'm waiting on a text from Flossy about Heldy."

Kitty tried to get the attention of her mother, who was deep in conversation with Coyne and Sir Alfred. Shrugging her shoulders, she turned to Finn. "It looks like everyone on the team has abandoned us. My mom used to be a chef at a casino, but I think it represents how many ways there are to cook eggs."

"Sure, Harvard, let's go with that."

"Time's up." Erin rang the bell. "Now, pass your answers to the table beside you, and let's see who is the winner tonight."

"Can't we just check our own answers?" Kitty asked Finn as he handed the sheet to the table to the left.

"Well, about three years ago, there was a Trivia Night and some cheating, drinking, and well, things got out of hand and there was a stabbing."

"A stabbing over Trivia?" Kitty couldn't help but laugh. "Sorry, not funny, but really, you guys take your Trivia pretty seriously."

"You have no idea. Isn't that right, Patrick?" Finn addressed a young lad barely out of his teens, who passed by collecting empty glasses.

"Ahhh, that's why they don't let me play anymore." Patrick wiped down the table with a dirty checkered rag.

"What was his part?" Kitty asked.

"He was the stabber and Erin was the stabee." Finn smiled as Kitty opened her mouth in disbelief. "But they are working in the same place. Did he go to jail?" She leaned closer to Finn so Patrick wouldn't hear.

"Nah, they settled it themselves and once they started dating, it all turned out for the best."

"Wait, so he stabbed her and now they're dating?"

"The heart wants what the heart wants. Besides, it wasn't a bad stab, it was more a poke with a pen, but my story sounds more exciting."

Kitty laughed. "Talk about having a bit of the Blarney in you."

"Indeed."

Chapter 22

1800s: KINGSTOWN, IRELAND

The rain lessened to a drizzle as William and Donal continued on their trek, stopping at a creek, the recent rain raising the level making it easier for the horse to drink. He lapped up the water, snorting through his nose, before lifting his tail and excreting. Without waiting to be told, William found sticks and pushed the foul-smelling horses discharge away from the water.

"Son, you are smart. I am glad you were privy to my conversation. We cannot have any animal dung near any water supply."

William glowed at his father's praise as they rehitched the horse and continued. The road was solitary but for the birds chirping in unison. William attempted to imitate the sounds and had a wren answer back. The horse kicked up the small stones on the road until Donal stopped the horse at a crossroads.

He led the horse up a small grade toward a mound of dirt covered with grass. Reminiscent of their sod cabin, except many times larger, William now sank to his bottom under an elm tree while the horse munched on the thigh-high grass.

"Father, why are we here?" William asked, looking over at the hill, and the surrounding countryside, at the fences. Some were laid with a mortar, while others were dry stones piled one on top of the other. "Why are the fences different?"

"So many questions, lad." Donal reached into the cart and handed William the bread. "We must make it last, but in answer to your questions. These fences were built by ancestors many, many years ago. Once we finish up, we will venture inside that mound. Now, these other fences, where the stones are laid one on top of the other were more recently built."

"Father, has our long walk gotten to you? How are we supposed to get inside a mound of dirt and why would we want to?" William managed to swallow a bit of the bread before his father cuffed him on the side of the read.

"Sorry, Father, I did not mean to disrespect you." William's eyes teared up, not so much at the pain of the hit but that his father was displeased with him.

"Everything I do, I do for our family." His father wiped his hand on his breeches and handed William a piece of the bread he was about to eat. "You will see where we are going and what we are doing, and you will share the experience with your own children one day." His father smiled. "Yes, one day you will be a father and a grand one at that."

"How can I not be, Father! Look at the example I have had." William stroked his father's hand, rich with blisters, blisters on top of blisters.

Standing up, William pulled his father to his feet. "Let us go and see this mound you speak of. It will indeed be an adventure for us."

"Indeed, and I will tell you the tale of my first visit to the mound when you were just a toddler."

Chapter 23

KITTY: NOW

"Looks like us folks from the colonies do know a thing or two." Kitty accepted the Trivia Night Trophy, which consisted of Erin's father's soccer trophy with his name scratched out and Trivia Night winner written over in black marker.

"It's been a pleasure. Who knew Harvard knew so much trivia. You're definitely on my team next week," Finn said as his phone buzzed, the ringer on loud to be heard over the clamor.

"Sorry, I gotta go. It's Flossy, and Heldy is in trouble."

"Is there anything I can do to help?" I asked, not knowing how I could assist but not wanting the night to end.

"Do you know anything about delivering a lamb?"Finn asked over his shoulder as he headed out the door.

"I don't know nothing about birthing no babies." I laughed when it appeared I was the only one who got the *Gone With The Wind* reference.

"Mom, I'm going with Finn." I grabbed my jacket and followed him, glad I had worn sensible shoes. I ran to catch up to him, bending over to catch my breath. I really did need to work out more, especially when we were on flat land in the village and hadn't approached any hills.

"Is it much further?" I asked, my question coming out in wheezes.

"Just around the corner. The barn is on the other side of the road, past the village." Finn said, his long legs one step to my four.

When I thought they would need to hook me up to oxygen, he stopped. "Shhh."

Sorry that my heavy breathing, my attempt to live was making too much noise, but as I regulated my gasping, I heard the moaning of the ewe.

Flossy met us at the barn door, the barnboards spaced so far apart, I could see inside. Even I could tell the ewe was in distress.

"Sorry to call you and interrupt your night." Flossy handed us each a pair of gloves. I put mine on wordlessly, unsure why they came all the way up my arms.

"No problem. Harvard won us the trophy. There's a lot of information floating around in that brain of hers."

Finn knelt beside Heldy and gently rubbed her nose, all the while making calming, soothing noises. "Heldy, will you let me help you? There you go, girl, you just relax and let me handle this for you. Harvard, can you come here and just pet her nose? She needs to be kept relaxed."

I replaced him at the head while he moved to the other end. Heldy tensed as I continued my chore.

"There's been no sign of the waterbags." Flossy gathered together soap, water, and a row of needles reminding me of a dentist's office.

With great care, Finn washed the area with soap and water, and used scissors to trim away some of the wool.

"Flossy, do you think Harvard has smaller hands than you?" Finn asked, hiding a smile. "If you think so, I'll need her to put her hand up here, cause mine's a bit too big to feel what I need to feel."

My stomach knotted at the thought.

Flossy grinned at my discomfort. "He's only kidding you. He likes this part the most, the birthing not the kidding, though he is a bit of a rascal."

"Okay, Heldy, it looks like your little one has decided to come out feet first. How you doing up there, Harvard?"

"Okay, better than Heldy, it seems." I tried to swallow, and breathe through my mouth. In for five breaths, hold for five, out for five.

"This is a piece of cake. I just have to pull the lamb out feet first, straight out, when a little dipsy doodle with changing the direction of the pull, and voila." Finn grinned. "Piece of cake. Oops, hang on a sec. I don't think she's done yet." Another head popped out of the vulva before Heldy let out a loud sigh and laid back down on the straw.

"Wow, twins." My stomach forgotten, my eyes now filled with tears. "I've never experienced the miracle of birth."

I watched Finn as he checked over the lambs, wiping each of them down with iodine. Heldy struggled to her feet and began to clean up her newborns.

"Would you like to feed them?" Flossy asked. She had retrieved a bottle from the small fridge on the other side of the barn.

"Good idea, Flossy. The second one will be able to use the tit on her own, but I think Harvard will need a bottle."

"Wait, do you have Guinness in the fridge? Yes, definitely I'll have one. Flossy, you think of everything." I definitely needed something.

"What I meant was I was thinking of calling the lambs Harvard and Yale. Harvard is the one who needs the bottle, the lamb, not you, but seeing how white your face is, I think it might be called for as well."

Heldy struggled to stand and began licking off the afterbirth.

"Well, thank you. I've never had anything named after me before. I get where you're getting the Harvard from, but why Yale?"

"Cause that's where I went to school," Finn said nonchalantly as he continued to tidy up and administer the various needles.

Chapter 24

1800s: BOYNE VALLEY, IRELAND

Elmville skittered across the top of the mound, skipping on his tippy toes to a beat only he could hear. With a wave of his shillelagh, the sky turned hazy from the recent rain. With another well-orchestrated shake, he produced a rainbow, the vibrant red, orange, yellow, green, blue, indigo, and violet, his biggest joy. Especially proud of how the rainbow ended at the top of the largest roof mound of the lot.

Elmville jumped about so proud of his artwork. A fortnight ago, he'd had worked on the Northern Lights and felt like he was an artist in the making. Never mind his brother Drurie, who played with the tides and the moons. Not very creative!!

Elmville sped around, twisting and twirling, throwing his hat up into the air. He reached into his pocket, removed his favorite coin and tossed it, running to catch it before flinging it up even higher. He slipped on the wet grass on the top of the mound, watching his coin fall down the side of the hillock, landing where the humans were.

"Look, Father, at the colors in the sky!" William shrieked like the toddler he was.

"It's called a rainbow and was created by the leprechauns. Legend has it that when you find the end of the rainbow, there will be a pot of gold." Donal thought of his own stupidity in bringing a toddler to Newgrange, but it was the winter solstice and not to be missed. Everyone should see it once in their lifetime and Edith agreed it was important for him to take William.

"Father, why are all these people here? Is everyone looking for the pot of gold?" William asked, tucking his hand into his father's.

A large hill stood majestically in front of them. To Donal's trained eye, it was about an acre in area. Grass covered the sides and roof where at the base corner stones ringed the mound. Movement caught the corner of Donal's eye at the crest of the mound, but when he looked again, nothing was there.

The rainbow so vibrant a few minutes ago, now faded, a mere memory.

William pointed at the sky. "Father, we won't be able to find the pot of gold."

An elderly man, bent over on a walking stick, his breath coming out in clouds with the cold air, said, "What foolhardiness you tell your boy! There's no such thing as a pot of gold at the end of the rainbow."

William removed his hand from his father's and crossed his arms over his chest. "If my father says such a thing exists, then it does."

"Well, young man," the man said, and coughed, spitting phlegm on William, "I've been on this earth a lot longer than you and I've never found it."

"You're not looking in the right place."

"Come along, William." Donal pulled his son away from the man and led him toward a cart displaying Galway shawls. "Which one do you think your mother would like?"

The shawls were fanned out on the wooden cart, the strong smell of wet sheep's wool emanating from the cart.

"What a lovely lad you have there, sir!" said the toothless crone, standing next to the cart. Her gray hair stuck out in all directions, and her red skirt reached brown well-worn leather shoes.

William moved closer to his father, further away from the old maid.

"William, do not be afraid. Now quit being silly and pick out one for your mother. I think she would like that one with the fringe. What do you think?"

William peeked around behind his father and reached for one which was hidden at the bottom, under the pile. The peddler held it up. It was a plain chestnut color at the top, the white and fawn colors weaved into an intricate pattern, ending at the different shades of fringe.

"Excellent choice, young man. Your lad has a good eye." She eyed the pair. "That will be three coins."

"I must buy my son food as well, and I'd like to get something for my daughter in addition." The vendor shrugged as Father walked away.

He hadn't made two strides when the woman ran after him, touching him on the shoulder.

"Sir, I have something for your daughter as well as your son. Let me show you." She nervously glanced over her shoulder as she led Donal and William away from the crowds.

"I made this for my own daughter, but she wasn't interested in something her mother made." She pulled out of the pocket of her red skirt a rag doll. Dressed in a miniature shawl, the doll had a happy expression on her face.

"Father, it looks like Susan." William pulled at Donal's hand.

"And what do you have for William?" Donal asked, all pretense of playing coy and trying to get her to lower her price.

From her other pocket, she withdrew a coin, tarnished and raw around the edges.

William's face dropped in disappointment. "Father, it's nothing but a dirty old coin. I bet I couldn't even buy anything with it."

The crone smiled, wrinkles creasing her brown, weathered face. "It is a leprechaun's coin. If you turn it over, you will see indented in it, the pot of gold as well as an etching of a rainbow."

"Father, is she telling the truth?" William asked, turning the coin in his hand, his eyes dancing as his face beamed.

"We will take all three for three coins," Father said, in a non-argumentative voice.

"Sold!" The woman wrapped the shawl and doll in newspaper. "Lad, hang on to that coin. Do not lose it or let anyone swindle it from you."

"Why would you sell a leprechaun's coin?" William asked. "Why not keep it for yourself?"

"I have all the luck I need; can't you tell?" The vendor cackled.

Elmville scootched over to the edge of the mound and watched the humans. He lost sight of the coin when it fell over the side. His chin sank dejectedly into his chest. He was in soooo much trouble. He had to find the coin.

The piece of gold, mined from Ross Island, protected a leprechaun from evil and balanced their own goodness and evilness. Without the coin, righteous would not be counted on the scales of justice. Devilish would become his strongest trait.

He had to retrieve the coin!!

Chapter 25

ANNIE: NOW

"Are you coming with us?" Annie asked Kitty as she changed her shirt for the fifth time.

"I don't want to be a gooseberry with you and Coyne," Kitty said, flipping through her phone. "Besides, I think I might go and visit Harvard and Yale. Did I tell you Finn is a vet, and he was trained at Yale? How cool is that?"

"Only about fifteen hundred times." Annie laughed. "Which looks better, the red sweater or the white?"

"Mom, you definitely need to get some clothes. You wore the white sweater last night, don't you remember? You did have a few Guinness," Kitty chastened her mother.

"I'll have you know I had some very interesting conversations with Coyne and his father. I was totally sober." Annie huffed.

"Sure, okay, you're preaching to the choir, Mom, but wear the red." Kitty glanced down at her phone. "Aren't you supposed to be meeting him at one p.m.? It's twelve fifty-eight."

"Bye, talk later. Sure you don't want to come with?" Mom asked as she ran out the door.

"You kids go and have fun. I'll just stay here with

the leprechauns and have a play date."

Annie found Coyne chatting with Flossy at the sign-in desk. Wearing a plaid shirt, the fabric rolled up to past his elbows, he took Annie's breath away. With his sunglasses tucked on the top of his head, he turned toward her, his eyes lazily glancing at her.

"Annie, we were just talking about you! On the original Coyne tour, was there anything on your bucket list for Ireland that's a must-see, or will you leave it to your tour guide?" Coyne reached over and removed a piece of lint from Annie's sweater. Her heart pulsed like she'd been hit with a defibrillator machine.

"Whatever anyone else wants to see, I'm easy. I mean, I'm good. I mean…" Heat flushed her face.

"You're the only one signed up for the Coyne tour, so your wish is my command." Coyne bowed. "But we can leave it to our own devices and see where the road takes us."

"Sounds good to me," Annie agreed, avoiding the smug look on Flossy's face.

"If we want to end up at the Leprechaun's Door for lunch, we'd better get a move on."

"Slan. Goodbye," Flossy said, waving as the pair left the lobby, heading out to the parking lot.

"Sorry, I wanted to borrow my dad's Tesla, but he had plans for today. Something about seeing a man about a horse." He grinned. "How lame is that at my age, needing to ask my dad to borrow his car? Good thing I moved out of the spare bedroom or I would be a real catch." He walked around and opened the car door for Annie, tucked her inside, then pulled his sunglasses down, walking around to the driver's side.

"All set," Annie said, putting on her sunglasses. "I

bet they don't sell many sunglasses in Ireland."

"That sounds like something your Kitty would say." He laughed.

"Sorry, it was somewhat rude of me. Sometimes my mouth opens before my brain starts up."

"Never you mind. Let me show you my country." He pulled out of the carpark, gravel spurting up. He adjusted the radio and lowered the volume, the light sounds of elevator music filling in the background.

"I would have taken you more of a WhiskeyAce fan." Annie tried to impress him with her knowledge of the Rock Celtic band.

"I do enjoy them, but it's early, maybe on the way home. Now, tell me all about Annie. We didn't get much of a chat done when we were at the pub. My father does like to control the conversation."

"Your father is lovely and gave me a lot of information. Now, if I can just remember what he told me. He was talking quite fast and with the noisiness in the bar, I could only pick up every other word."

"I'm sure he'd be happy to go over it again with you. Nothing he likes better than talking to pretty ladies." He pulled over into a cobblestone parking lot. "We'll park here and do some walking. Are you fine to walk? There are a few hills."

Still glowing from his comment, Annie surveyed the shops she'd only had a glimpse at on her way to the pub. Stores pushed up against the road, and only one side of the road provided a sidewalk. Hanging baskets, hung on metal rails, spilled forth with trailing ivy feathering the ground. Red-painted barrels lined the road like Royal Soldiers, planted with geraniums. Pink, yellow, and white pansies overflowed window boxes.

Not to be outdone, an attached cottage had so many blooms they cascaded onto the road. It was like walking into a nursery. Annie sneezed as she caught a whiff of all the flowers at once.

"Bless you." Coyne grabbed her arm, leading her past the flowers. "I forget some people need to build up a tolerance to the scents." He sneezed. "I guess it doesn't matter how long you've lived here, if the wind blows the wrong way, you have an allergic reaction."

"It's beautiful." Annie stopped to take a picture.

Across the street behind parked cars was a convenience store, peeling stickers in the window. A green post office pillar box stood like a sentinel out front. Nestled beside was the store Annie wanted to visit. "Do you mind if we stop here?"

Without waiting for an answer, Annie pushed the door open, inhaling the scent of lavender and lemongrass.

Bright yellow and purple paint drew her eye to the wall at the back of the store where elaborate curtains hung on rails separating the store from the changing rooms.

"Coyne Tobin, what brings you to our fine establishment today? Are you in need of a new shirt? We have some lovely ones, or perhaps something a little fancier? You do have a lady with you, you need to sharpen yourself up a tad." The teenage girl with a nose ring reminded Annie of a bull. She swatted his arm. "I'm Sion. How can I help you?"

"Would you mind if I had a gander?" Annie asked, taking in the throne-like red velvet chair beside a row of shoes, many still in boxes.

"Annie is from America, so she's learning our

ways." Coyne flopped down in a yellow plush chair, and propped his sunglasses back on his head.

"Surely you must have charity shops in America?" Sion asked, leaning against a rack jammed with sweatpants.

"That we do." Annie mused at the variety of pants, sweaters, and tie-dye shirts. One particularly caught her attention, a florescent pink. "Kitty would love this."

"Would you like me to take it to the cash while you continue shopping?" Sion asked, picking at a nail while she waited for a response.

"Yes. I'm looking for something warm. I live in Las Vegas so I didn't pack a lot of warm clothes. Do you have any suggestions?"

"If you follow me, we just got in a Galway shawl. It does smell a bit musty but I have some spray that will take care of that." Sion led her to a pile of cardboard boxes perched like a wobbling tower about to fall over. "Coyne, your father dropped these off this morning so, no offense meant about the smell, but there are some really dote items in here. Sorry, dote means cute. Coyne, have you taught the girl nothing?"

Annie and Sion began to nose through the boxes, tossing clothes to the left, which warranted further investigation, and others to the right they had no intention of wasting their time with. "Your father did a lot of purging."

"It was time," Coyne said, amused at Annie as she sat, legs crossed around the smallest of the boxes.

"I knew there was one in here." Sion held up the brown fringed Galway shawl. "Coyne, I remember seeing pictures of your great-grandmother wearing this, the sod cabin in the background.

"She was a true lady. She would tell tales about leprechaun gold and Newgrange. She was quite the storyteller." Sion wrapped the shawl around Annie's shoulders and took a smell. "I'll spray some of our scents onto the shawl and you'll be as right as rain."

"I'm taking Annie to Newgrange when we finish up here." Coyne glanced at his watch. "Any other treasures you'll be looking at before we leave?"

Annie rooted through the box, digging out a pair of silver Celtic knot clip-on earrings, a matching bracelet, a locket, and a sweater of thick sheep's wool. "Oh, this looks warm."

"Coyne, she's got a good eye. Ireland is known for that type of jumper. It's an Aran jumper and the style you're looking at is one of the original. It was worn by Coyne's great-grandmother, and it's the real deal. Not like so many of the ones you'll see at boot sales. It's in the natural colors of the sheep, and the way it was processed, it retained its oils. It's waterproof, which as you know, it is a tad rainy here.

"Is there anything else made of sheep's wool or something sheep-related? Kitty helped deliver a lamb, well, actually two last night with Finn, so I'd like to get her something else, as well."

"How about this?" Sion held up a sweatshirt with a picture of sheep and the saying, I love ewe. The body of the sheep was actual sheep's wool. "It's a tad on the tacky side, but I would love it if my mom got it for me."

"You know what, I think I'm going to keep looking, but add it to my pile, anyway." Annie got out her wallet, adding the earrings and bracelet to the pile. "I think I'm done."

Coyne sighed. "Good thing. I was thinking I would need to get a trailer for all your purchases. Sion, are you sure there's nothing you'd like out of those boxes before the sale goes through?"

"I'm good." Sion busied herself behind the counter, avoiding everyone's eyes.

"Ha-ha, obviously you haven't gone shopping with a female for a while. I think you got off easy, don't you, Sion?" Annie handed over her credit card when she noticed a flask. "Add this on, please," Annie whispered to Sion.

With the stealthiness of Houdini, Sion wrapped the flask in tissue paper and grabbed another sheet for the jewelry before carefully folding the shawl, sweater, and shirt for Kitty in a reusable cloth bag. She handled the items as if they were purchases from Tiffany's.

"Thanks for all your help, Sion. You've been a gem, and to thank you for your help, I bought this for you." Annie handed her the I Love Ewe sweater.

"Really, for me? Coyne, a complete stranger is nicer to me than you are, and you've known me a lot longer."

Sion ran around from behind the counter and gave Annie a big hug, squeezing the air out of her lungs.

"I'm nice to you. Don't I give you a place to live?"

"Well, gee, don't you think it's the least a father can do for his daughter?" Sion grinned as she held the door open for them. "Have fun at Newgrange, and don't pick up any leprechaun coins."

Back out in the sunlight, Coyne wore his sunglasses. "So, we'll head up to Newgrange via Dun Laoghaire, and depending on the time, we'll stop for lunch at the Leprechaun's Door or we might just have to find a spot on the way."

Annie stowed her purchases in the back seat of the car, pulling the shawl out and wrapping it around her shoulders, inhaling the bouquet of the fresh spray. Climbing into the car, she turned and grinned at Coyne. "So, you have a daughter?"

Chapter 26

1800s: IRELAND

Donal and William ensured their horse was watered and fed before joining the queue, which wrapped around the base of the curved stones. Torches were lit around the circumference of the dome and several men used the warmth from the flames to warm their hands.

Ornate stone doors secured the entrance as the men pushed forward to get inside into some semi-warmth.

"Father, what is so important inside this grass house?" William asked, his coin tucked tightly in his hand, shoved into the pocket of his breeches.

"Son, you will see, just be patient." Before the words were out of Donal's mouth, the sun poked from behind the clouds. The visitors were silenced as the spectacle unfolded in front of their very eyes. Farmers without the use of metal tools had created the event before them. The Sun slid down the hallway, a hallway in perfect alignment with the travels of the sun during this special night. For seventeen minutes they stood, everything forgotten as the sun illuminated the walls and floor, creating a glowing rectangle.

Elmville, hidden behind one of the rocks left in place by a glacier, was silenced by the light show. He took his cap off in respect to the marvel.

As quickly as it came, it disappeared. Donal and William, fortunate enough to make it inside, continued to walk through the tunnel lined by boulders twice as tall as Donal.

A gleam caught William's eye, and he bent down and picked it up, tucking it into his pocket alongside the one the woman had given him. There was just enough room for them to turn around and join the rope of men heading back outside.

"What was that, Father? What did we just witness?" William asked, now wise beyond his toddler years. "It was the sun as I have never seen it. It was magical."

"It was indeed, son." Donal led him over to the horse. "Now we must get back on the road, son, to get back to your mother and Susan."

"Father, I have something for you." William pulled out the piece of rectangular gold he had recently found and handed it to him. "Father, I have the other coin. I'd like you to have this one. It's not a coin, but like a crow, I like shiny objects."

"Son, you don't know what luck this piece of gold will bring us, but I can assure you it will." Donal hugged William. "No idea, son."

Chapter 27

KITTY: NOW

"How are the patients doing?" I asked, as I walked into the barn sneezing,the smell of straw catching me unawares.

Finn sat on an overturned milk bucket, the sun shining through the open slates in the barnboards. "Yale and Harvard are doing amazing. I don't think I ever thanked you for your help with the delivery."

"I don't think I was much help. All I did was keep Heldy calm while you did all the hard work." I stooped to stroke the face of Heldy as the two lambs baaaed, wanting my attention. I left the mother and used each hand to caress the pair.

"Don't sell yourself short. The most important thing is to keep the mother calm. If she panics, it stresses her heart as well as the lambs, and we could have had three dead animals on our hands."

I shivered, not wanting to think of what might have been. "What are you doing now?"

"The lambs have to have powered colostrum, so Flossy mixed some up and I'm going to give it to them in the bottle, unless you'd like to?" He grinned, walking to the small fridge and handing her the bottles. "Forget I even asked. Here you go."

"Not that I mind, but can't Heldy give this to the

lambs?"

"It's kinda hard for her to hold the bottles." Finn laughed. "When one of the ewes has twins, I like to supplement with bottle as well, just to ensure there's enough."

"Makes sense." I perched on a bale of hay and proceeded to bottle-feed the lambs. "So, what made you get into the vet/shepherd field? You must really like sheep."

"Vets look after more than sheep, but living here, it does seem mostly the animals I deal with. Tip the bottle a little more on an angle so Harvard gets less air.We don't want her to be full of hot air."

"Ha ha." I snuck a glance at Finn to find him watching me. I leant toward him as his eyes lowered and I screamed.

A mouse ran from the bale I was sitting on, up my leg, along the top of the bale, escaping. hiding in the fresh raked straw. Sticking its nose and whiskers out, it fastened me with a beady glare as it's whiskers flickered.

I shrieked and jumped on top of another turned-over metal bucket. Finn was doubled over in laughter, holding his stomach as Heldy looked on. I didn't know a sheep could have an amused look, but she did.

"It's not funny. I hate mice." My eyes darted around the barn, piercing anything moving. The wide slots between the barnboards caused a breeze to factor inside the barn, so it didn't help that the chaff from the hay sifted.

"Mice are a fact of life with farm life," Finn commented as another mouse scurried from the opposite side.

I looked for something higher to climb onto and saw a ladder, but to get to it I would have to walk across the lava floor.

I would be forever stuck on the bucket. I would live and die on the bucket. I didn't have much going on with my life anyway, but I hadn't planned to spend it standing on a bucket in a barn in Ireland.

Like I was a bag of grain, Finn walked over and threw me over his shoulder. "I'll rescue you, fair maiden. I'll get you to safety away from the vicious and evil mice." He carried me across the floor, my attention back to the floor, not enjoying the strength of his arms, and the smell of his woodsy aftershave, intermingled with straw, and for some reason, fresh morning dew.

Mice might be okay after all. Maybe Finn was my *the one*. I had to text Ben.

Finn dropped me gently in front of the barn doors. "Do you think you can make it from here?"

The barn doors pushed open. An angel with the sun highlighted behind him stood before us. Finn and I chorused as one: "Ben! What are you doing here?"

"Finn, is it really you?"

Chapter 28

1800s: KINGSTOWN, IRELAND

Edith, Susan tucked tightly in her arms, rushed from the doorway of the sod cabin when they heard the familiar clickity clack of the family cart.

"Oh, husband, I'm so glad you are back safe and sound. William, was it an adventure with your father?" She handed Susan over to Donal and grasped William in a hug, like she would never let him go.

"We saw the winter soldiers," William said as he rustled in the back of the cart for the gifts.

"Let me get the horse settled." Donal patted her on her rear flank. He led her toward a makeshift barn. "She got us there and back, saved us a lot of wear and tear on our shoes."

Susan tugged at her brother's breeches. "Mother, I cannot wait to show you the gifts we brought you and yes, sister, we didn't forget you either."

Donal came back inside the sod cabin, his arms filled with bundles of items.

"William, would you like the honor of handing out the gifts?"

"Susan, this is for you." William handed her the doll. "We thought you would like this since it had the same hair color as you do. Red tomato."

"William, be nice to your sister. I must say, while I

missed you, son, I did not miss the bickering." Edith smiled to take the spikiness away from her words.

"Mother, I picked this out for you. It was hidden at the bottom of the pile." William handed his mother the shawl and then took it and wrapped it around her shoulders. "It's called a Galway shawl and it will keep you warm, mother."

"William, husband, what a thoughtful gift. I shall wear it forever. I will not mind getting up to stoke the fire with such a blanket around my shoulders. It's so much nicer than the one I have now." She shucked it off and wrapped the new one around her.

She raised her shoulders in anticipation, the warmth from the shawl already creeping through her bones.

"Husband, tell me all about your adventure. Did you receive what you sought?" Edith pulled both William and Susan into her lap, covering them both with the sides of the shawl.

"But I did not tell you the best part. When father and I were in Newgrange, I found a leprechaun coin *and* a piece of gold." William dug deep into the pocket of his breeches and pulled out the bounty for all to see.

"You are a liar. That is not a coin from a leprechaun." Susan took the coin from him, surveying it. "Is it, mother?"

Edith's hand heated when William placed both pieces in her palm. Taking stock first of the coin, she flipped it over and viewed the rainbow. Next, she surveyed the oblong piece of gold, glancing at Donal, barely able to hold her smile. "You have a wise son."

"I agree, wife. I wanted you to see it first. We must hide it somewhere safe and we will use them when we need them."

"Agreed, husband, we must be careful as we do not want word to get out." Edith glanced down at her shawl and grinned. She pushed her children off her lap and went to her knitting basket. With the practice and skill her mother taught her, without delay, she snatched up her knitting needles, and with cream-colored yarn, she ran up seven rows in a garter stitch, finishing off with a flourish. With a darning needle in hand, she attached the completed product to the inside of her shawl. "No safer place husband than next to my bosom."

"We will see about that." He smiled the smile of a man who was indeed in love with his wife.

Chapter 29

ANNIE: NOW

Coyne drove them along the shoreline of Dun Laoghaire, one hand on the steering wheel, the other pointing out the sights. "Due to the weather and shipwrecks, Dun Laoghaire has a manmade harbor where vessels can take refuge to wait out the storms. Over to the left is the King George monument erected when he came to visit."

"That pavilion looks like a Mississippi Riverboat," Annie said, catching Coyne's enthusiasm for the town.

"Good eye. Yes, that was the town's folk intention way back in the 1800s, and if you look out the window, well now behind us is the Carnegie Library. We were fortunate the man liked to spend his money and we were the welcome recipients.

"Over there, where now the row of stores stand, was the home of the pub, The Royal Sea Lion." Coyne waved his hand again like he was in an orchestra.

"Did they have Trivia Night there too?" Annie asked, her head on a swivel as she attempted to keep up with the directions he was pointing.

"Not that I know of because they were on strike."

"Wait, a bar in Ireland on strike, that couldn't have been good for business. Tell me the story!" She reached out to touch his arm, the soft hairs feather-like to her fingers.

"Back in 1939, the owner of The Royal Sea Lion fired his unionized employee and replaced him with a female non-unionized one. I guess he figured she was easier on the eyes and probably thought of his bottom line or her bottom line." Coyne signaled, made a left turn, and continued, "Well, the other staff didn't take too kindly, and they all went out on strike."

"Then what happened?" Annie settled back in the seat, content to listen to his voice, his accent filling the car.

"Well, Irishmen are known to be stubborn, must be the red hair, so neither side would give. The employees would picket outside the doors; this went on for thirteen years. Someone said the number of miles they picketed would have amounted to close to forty-one thousand miles. The original players left to find other employment."

"I guess they got tired of walking." Annie chuckled.

"So, WWII came along and in March of 1943, a German U-boat stopped the Irish Elm ship. The weather wasn't the best so they had to yell across the waters. One of the sailors happened to mention he was from Dun Leoghaire, to which one of the Germans asked if the strike at the bar was still on." He grinned like a Cheshire cat. "I kid you not."

Annie held her sides, she was laughing so hard. "Okay, I need to find a bathroom. Your stories should come with disclaimers. I wonder if the war might have been over sooner if the strike had settled when the U-boat was in these waters. The Germans might have come on land for some beer."

"Good point, I hadn't thought of that. The strike only settled because the landlord got a great offer on the land."

Coyne parallel parked into a spot in front of The Failte. "Washroom is to the right inside the door. You go and I'll grab us a table."

Annie nodded her thanks, and yanked open the door, heading inside, brushing shoulders with an elderly lady who was leaving.

"Annie, is that you?" The woman dressed like she was attending an afternoon tea party with the queen, grabbed her arm holding her.

"Hi, Mildred. Wait here, I'll be right back." Annie rushed past, pushed open the door, and heaved a sigh of relief when her bottom hit the porcelain.

Washing her hands, she glanced at the mirror. "What the heck was Mildred Hutchings doing in Dun Laoghaire?"

Using the paper towel, Annie pulled open the heavy red-painted door, her hands not touching the long brass handle to find Coyne sitting at the table closest to the door, waving to attract her attention. Mildred hovered at the bar like a drunk with her last pound note, adjusting her blue hat, the peacock feather dancing in the wind every time the door opened.

"Annie, I hoped I'd get to see you." Mildred hugged her, the mask she wore only covering her mouth, not her nose.

"I thought you had Covid." Annie held up a finger to Coyne, as he smirked, no choice but to overhear the conversation.

"Nope, a mixup in the results. That's the Clinic for you. Normally you can get the results while you wait, but they were trying a different system. And you wonder why people hesitated to get the needle. Not me, though. I thought that's why they do testing to make it safe for people like me. Though I didn't share with Ben I had received the needle ahead of time. When it was discovered I didn't have Covid, I got the booster before I left." Mildred patted her own arm. "It is a tad sore, but I said to Ben,'Ben, let's hop on a plane and hopefully we can meet up with Annie and Kitty' and look, here you are." She leaned closer to Annie. "Don't look now, but there's a handsome man trying to catch our eye. Blimey, I just arrived in this country and already the men are hitting on me. Must be the hat. A good hat never goes out of style. Do you know I wore this hat to the Queen's Coronation? Oops, I shouldn't say that too loud."

"Are you afraid people will hear how old you are?" Annie asked, always wanting to rub salt in any wound Mildred might have.

"No, but in Ireland they aren't too fond of the Monarchy. I heard tell they don't even like monarch butterflies."

"It is a rarity for them to show up here and we like the British just fine. An old wives tale." Coyne said from the table. "Annie, do you and your friend want to join me?"

"Blimey! He's even better looking up close." Mildred strode across the room to the table like she was in a 100-meter dash, sliding into the booth beside Coyne. "And what is your name, young fellow, and how do you know Annie?" Without taking a breath, she yelled, "Barkeep. Barkeep, can I have a beer? Any kind." She turned her attention back to Coyne. "Well, are you going to answer me or keep me in the dark?"

"Coyne, this is Mildred, Mildred, Coyne. Coyne is giving me a tour of the town, and we have a tight time frame, so we can't stay long."

"I'm going to order us a beer. Would you ladies like some pub food, like fries or a bag of crisps?" Coyne asked, a bemused look hijacking his face.

"I think I'm good with just the beer," Mildred said. "I have to keep this girlish figure or the boys won't be looking at me. I hear celebrities like to frequent this area and I'd like to catch myself a rich one."

"So how was your flight?" Annie asked when Coyne was away at the bar. "I heard Ben lost his job but landed on his feet."

"Benny always lands on his feet. He should be in Cirque du Soleil." Mildred gulped down her beer and waved at Coyne. She held up and pointed to the empty glass whereas he understood the sign language and nodded.

"True, I wish Kitty would find her life's passion. Her advertising degree isn't worth the paper it's printed on for all the good it does her. I don't think you ever stop worrying about your kids, no matter how old you or they get." Annie nodded her thanks when Coyne returned to the table with their drinks and took a sip, wiping off her foam mustache with a napkin.

"True that. I know Benny was heartbroken on the plane in a real funk, but I said 'Benny, if she's meant to be, she's meant to be.'" Turning her focus back onto Coyne, she continued. "Coyne, what an unusual name! Are you married?"

Coyne, choking on his beer, began to cough, raising the attention to the other patrons.

"Always knew Coyne couldn't handle his beer." Laughed one, slapping the other on the back. "Just like his old man, he smelled beer and was drunk."

"Pipe down all of you," Mildred ordered. "Coyne is a nice young man and it would do you all good and well to be nice to him."

The eldest of the men removed his poor boy cap and bowed to Mildred. "Our apologies, mamam. We have known Coyne since he was in his mother's womb and some of us even longer."

"Well, I truly doubt that." Mildred huffed. "I don't need to be made fun of. I'm an American visiting your fine country and am due some respect."

"Mildred, it's okay, let it go," Coyne suggested. "And it's true, he was my mother's doctor."

Mildred drowned her embarrassment in her beer in an attempt to hide the blush rising on her face.

"You're not married?" Mildred turned the conversation back onto Coyne. "How can such a handsome man as you not be married?"

"He does have a daughter," Annie added as she was curious as to his backstory. It seemed every time she got closer to hearing it, something or someone interrupted them.

"True, I do have a daughter. Her name is Sion and she works at the charity shop where Annie almost bought out the store."

"Really? Was there a lot of good buys there?" Mildred asked, almost forgetting her interrogation of Coyne.

"There was! It was better than a Boxing Day Sale."

"Oh, I'm going to have to stop there. But before I forget, what about Sion's mother—where is she in the

124

picture?" Mildred asked like a dog with a bone and the sooner Coyne learned this, the easier it would be on everyone.

He uttered six words silencing the pub.

"She was killed by a leprechaun."

Chapter 30

1800s: IRELAND

"Father, will we be seeing the summer soldiers?" William asked his father as the horse and cart continued on its way from the sod cabin toward the sea.

"It's the wrong time of year for that. This trip is more of a business deal. We're going to see some men about land and produce."

"Father, I'd like to stop by Newgrange. Would it be possible? I was very lucky the last time we were there and I think my luck might continue." William crossed his arms over his chest, tightening his brown jacket. Although it was spring, there was a dampness in the air. He was fortunate his father was a man who didn't want his son to wear a dress like his friends had to. It really wasn't practical in the fields.

"Will my son and I be allowed to visit Newgrange on the morrow?" Father asked a young man, his belongings wrapped in a checkered cloth, attached to a stick, slung over his shoulder.

The man shrugged his shoulders, his stick bobbing, continuing on his way.

"He's not too friendly," William commented to his father, even their horse snorting at the man's rudeness.

"You never know the burdens some people carry. They are not always visible. One of my father's favorite sayings was: It's often a person's mouth that breaks his nose and another one was every man is sociable until a cow invades his garden."

William sat back against the padded backrest of the cart, an upgrade on the conveyance, pondering his father's words. "Father, if a man is walking with his belongings, do you believe he owns a garden?"

"Perhaps he's not as fortunate as we are, son. If it wasn't for your keen eye, we wouldn't have the luxury of the gold piece." He glanced around to ensure no one was near them. Reaching into his shirt pocket, he unwrapped a handkerchief containing gold filings. "Son, watch and learn."

Donal tucked it back into his pocket as they drew closer to the port. Ships whistles blew and boomed every minute. William, trying to take in everything at once, rubbed the kink out of his neck, the same soreness when Susan grabbed the blanket and his neck was exposed all night to the cold. Rich and vibrant reds, oranges, and blues reminded William of a moving rainbow as the women swelled onto the docks, the ships waiting like bookends at the piers. The older women holding onto wide-brimmed hats, protection of the wind from the bay causing havoc with hair, hats, and dresses. Younger girls, not so wise to the way of the wind, chased down their hats, some crying as they flew off into the bay, floating in the sun, before sinking like potatoes in the water.

Donal jumped off the cart, drawing the horse toward the stables. He handed a stable hand a coin, as they headed toward the bay. Bypassing the collections of families, Donal beelined toward a man who stood off by himself.

"Edward Collins, as I live and breathe." Donal grasped the man's hand and then engaged him in an elaborate embrace. "Fancy meeting you here on these docks. Are you heading overseas?"

Edward gave a dismissive nod, then turned his back on Donal, who with great confidence walked to where the man faced.

"I have an offer for you. I know you are a busy man, so I'll be quick. The lands you currently own, I'm assuming you will have no need for them as you are leaving."

"What is my business isn't your business? Go away." Edward attempted to light up a cigarette, but the wind kept blowing out the matchstick until Donal cupped his hands. Edward puffed greedily.

"I will purchase your lands." Donal moved a few steps to the left, as the wind had shifted and the smoke was blowing in his face.

"And how can you afford my lands?" Edward exhaled, coughing into the air. "Though I do have the deeds on me."

"Don't worry about my affairs. What do you believe would be a fair market price for the land?" Donal asked, his fingers playing with the gold shavings in his pocket.

Edward and Donal managed to haggle down a price and shook hands, the deeds exchanging hands with a portion of the gold.

"Your father is a good negotiator," Edward admitted. "Though I have to ask, what are you planning on growing there?"

"Potatoes!"

"Come along, son. We have one more person to

meet up with." Donal, strutting along like he was the cock of the walk, stopped at a gaggle of men, sea shipmen who stood smoking by the door of the largest of the vessels.

"I was told to meet Brion." Donal stopped suddenly, William running into the back of his father.

"I'm Brion." Hands behind his back, the sailor's face was lined and sunburned, the skin peeling pink in places. Red hair haloed around the navy blue cap, a green scarf at his neck.

"May we talk without an audience?" Donal shook the man's hand and waved him over.

"Nah, there is nothing you will say to me that my mates cannot hear." Brion puffed out his chest. "Who told you to ask for me?"

Donal ignored his question. "I'm looking to buy some potatoes."

Laughter erupted amongst the group of me. "Look around you, sir. All these people are jumping on ships to leave Ireland and potatoes and you're looking to buy some to plant." Glancing down at William, the sailor patted him on the head. "Boy, I hope you got your brains from your mother's side of the family, cause you'll be in trouble if it's from your father's."

William clenched his jaw as he ground out the words from between clenched teeth. "Listen to my father and you might learn a thing or two."

"Why you little wise guy! I outta!" Brion held up his hand to calm his friend.

"Okay, so let's talk. Obviously, you don't want the lumpers." Brion bit his lip as he raised his eyebrows. "Whoever sent you to me, knows I have the best produce."

"Exactly, that's why I'm here talking to you. I've acquired some land, and want to get them planted as soon as I'm back. I'm looking for thirty sacks."

"I can give you twenty-five and I'll throw in some carrots, beets, and cabbage." Donal nodded and Brion sent his mates to retrieve the sacks from the ship's hold.

Brion surveyed the gold filings and tipped them into his pouch. "You never see gold nowadays. How did you come across it?"

Donal glanced over at the sailor who had given William such a hard time. "My son. He is a smart one. He got the looks from my wife and the brains from me. William, go and fetch the horse and cart, so we can load up the sacks."

William nodded, both bored with the grown-ups' talk and his father bragging of how smart he was, walked up the short hill away from the docks.

"Elizabeth, stay away from the horses." William turned to see a girl about his age, her hair tied with ribbons, her dress the color of a newborn chick, bend over backward to walk under the horse. He had never seen such a feat. Aware she had an audience, she jumped up on top of the animal and stood upright, her shoes balancing her.

"You belong in the circus." William smiled as he watched her do a handstand. The horse, it seemed, was as much in awe and startled as William.

"Elizabeth, how many times have I told you not to stand? You foolish girl, you're going to fall and break your neck." Her mother stood hands on hips, her voice edged in tension.

"Mother, I'm fine. I'm an expert." The words were no more out of her mouth when the horse, spooked by the whistle of a steamship, bolted, causing her to spin off. Instead of a practiced dismount, she landed on her bottom, her once pristine yellow dress now covered with horse manure and cobblestone dust.

William burst out laughing, attempting to hide his laughter behind his hand.

Elizabeth took a handful of manure and threw it overhand, landing at William's feet.

"I believe you to be a much better horsewoman than a thrower of manure, but not by much." He bent down and bobbed as she continued to bombard him with pelts of anything within arms reach.

"Elizabeth Doyle, stop that right now. You are a lady and prey tell it's time you started acting like one and not a common street hussy." Her mother's nose was wrinkled in disgust.

"Elizabeth Doyle, that's a name I won't forget." William accepted the reins of his horse from the stable hand and headed back toward the docks. "Elizabeth Doyle, you've got spunk."

Elizabeth stuck her tongue out at him as she raised her hand to throw a rock at his head before her mother grasped her arm and smacked her behind, Elizabeth's anger turning to pain.

Chapter 31

KITTY: NOW

"Ben, I can't believe you're here?" The mouse forgotten, I squeezed Ben tighter than I had anyone ever."Wait, why are you here? Oh no, did Mildred die? I'm so sorry. Are you okay?"

I hugged Ben again, my eyes reddening from the tears. "I know how much you loved your mother."I turned to Finn. "Mildred was Ben's mom and she always wore a hat."

"Kitty, she's not dead. Well, maybe the townspeople have lynched her, but she didn't die from Covid. It was a misdiagnosis, and well, you know my mother. She has the letter, proudly shown to every customs officer, homeland security officer, and cab driver from Vegas to here," Ben explained, using his thumb to wipe away her tears. "Hi, Finn."

"Hi, Ben, how's Smokey?" Finn picked up a piece of straw and began chewing it.

"Wait, you two know each other? How do you two know each other? You know Smokey?" I ignored the mouse running across the highest bale of hay.

"Finn was in Vegas," Ben said. "We met at Vegas Toppers and he came back to my place and was introduced to Smokey."

"Sure, you introduce Finn to Smokey but not me."

I stuck my hands on my waist and narrowed my eyes with suspicion. "Were you trying to keep Finn away from me?"

"Can we move on? Obviously, Finn wasn't as interested as I thought he was, so my mistake." He ambled away, inadvertently stepping on a pitchfork, which shot up, the wooden handle clocking him in the forehead."

"I'm fine, let's go." Ben nudged away the concern, the redness haloing an already forming bruise.

"Ben, quit being stubborn. Let Finn have a look at it. He's a doctor."

"Doctor? You told me you were a shepherd? Wonder what else you lied about?" Ben rubbed his forehead, pulling open the barn doors. "I'm walking back to town."

"I'm a vet and I can explain." Finn sent me a sideways glance. "Is he always this stubborn?"

"Pretty much but wait until you meet his mother."

Chapter 32

ANNIE: NOW

Coyne made an extravagant glance at his watch. "We'd better get going if you want to make Newgrange before it closes."

"I guess that's my hint," Mildred said, finishing up the rest of her beer.

"I'll use the washroom." Annie stood up. "Mildred, are you coming?"

"No. Surprisingly, I have a steel bladder. I'm like a camel." She blushed when she was approached by one of the men who had been seated at the bar.

He bowed and removed his baseball cap. "I would be honored to show you around the town."

"I don't go out with men I don't know." Mildred fluffed her hat and pulled at the cuffs of her jacket.

"Allow me to introduce myself. I'm Sir Alfred."

Chapter 33

1800s: IRELAND

"Brion, it has been a pleasure to do business with you." Donal shook the man's hand as they gazed upon the bounty loaded onto the wagon. "We're going to head home and get this bounty planted, but one question for you. My son wanted to visit Newgrange again, as we had stopped in for the Winter Solstice when he was a youngster. Such a magnificent sight."

Brion focused on Donal, then threaded his way through the crowd and stopped to chat with a group of men who all turned toward Donal as one and nodded. Brion walked back toward William and his father and whispered, "Go to Newgrange tonight. Both of you. There is a ceremony those men have agreed you can attend. It will be life-changing."

****

William, anticipating the mood of foreboding, was quiet as his father tied the horse and cart to the hitching post, the sacks hidden.

"Over here and put these on," a thick Irish brogue ordered.

"Watch and stay silent. Your horse and goods will be safe here. Return these items here and we expect you to attend every year on this date." He waved them to follow him, and William slipped his hand inside his father's as they walked into Newgrange.

Midcentury black iron sconces held thick candles. Their flames danced against twelfth-century stone walls. Dampness filled the subterranean cellar as the cloaked beings gathered at each point of a pentagram, around a stone table stained and rubbed smooth by past events. Humming rather than chanting filled the air. Twenty minutes past the hour, torches surrounding the altar flicked to life as the murmurs modified to a low-grade whistle. The beings shifted their positions from the points of the pentagram. Each knelt on one knee in front of the altar, while the other leg was stretched to the left, the stance learnt in centuries past to better balance.

As the light brightened on the altar, the beings made the sign of a pentagram on the front of their crimson-colored robes, all but one who wore brown. Their heads bowed, they slowly rose to their full height.

The tallest of the beings stepped forward and broke the silence, his words slightly slurred. "Let us live in relevance. What can give us life can so easily take it away. We must honor and support the power so history does not repeat itself." His virgin wool robe, taken from several of his lambs' first shearing, was attached around his neck with a clasp of copper and silver, mined locally centuries ago. The train of the robe stretched to each of the points of the pentagram, covering the bare feet of each of the beings. He did not have an accent common to the area, but nonetheless, he was easy to understand.

"Let us rejoice in what we have conquered and we will spread the wealth." From the long sleeve of his robe, he withdrew a slate bowl as the humming began again, the tempo rising as the candles flickered. He raised his voice to be heard. "Blood is the mainstay to each God's creatures, whether two-legged, four-legged, flying or ground-bound. We must celebrate the blood, our ancestry, our lineage."

With an unknown force, the flames leaping against the walls were extinguished one by one, leaving the only light by the altar.

He placed the porringer on a small shelf by the altar.

The humming silenced as a goat was tugged into the room, pulling at the rope, almost as if he could sense his fate.

The beings lifted the goat onto the stone table. Each had a specific position to hold the animal still. As one, the humming began, causing the goat to strain.

"Little one, do not be scared," the being whispered soothingly to the animal. Whether it was the words or exhausted by the fight, the beast laid back on the table. As the beings were no longer needed to restrain the animal, they stepped back, leaving the being with the brown robe alone at the table.

In a short while, the goat was slaughtered. One of the beings held the bowl to catch the blood and a quick knife slice secured the animal's liver which was also added to the basin.

William's face and demeanor were glacial, so used was he to farm life and the butchering of animals for human want.

With a nod, from east to west, each of the beings stepped forward and took a bite from the raw liver, before handing it onward to the next.

"Let what we have created on this day and the

worship we have pronounced here, let no man put asunder." The head being raised the bowl to his lips, drank it in one gulp, and then consumed the remainder of the liver. Flicking his robe out of his way, he hastened toward the altar, bowing as he walked. The humming began again, stronger now the iron from the liver was ingested into the beings. When he reached the altar, he wrapped his hands around the deity, and poured the remaining blood over the top.

"Here I share with you the lifeblood, so you may prosper and continue to grow."

Flames flickered from the torches, and a green glow emanated from the deity. Many eyes illuminated from the idol, each focusing on one of the beings, before dimming from green to darkness.

Each of the beings bowed, and retreated their steps, following the path from which they had originally entered.

The last being retreated, then felt an electrical jolt as the idol simmered. The green eyes began to charge, focusing on the back of the last being, charging into him as the eyes once again dimmed, now fully drained.

With his head bowed, William concentrated on not tripping over the robe which dragged onto the ground. Intent on following the crowd, he hung back, the crowd narrowing in front of him. Gawking in disbelief, he saw tucked into crevices human bones, different from animal bones so common around the fields, black and burned. One remained unfired, the bones as white as the rocks surrounding it. Precious stones marked the tomb. William stumbled to catch up to the men, his heart hammering as he put as much distance as he could between the skeletons and himself.

Chapter 34

COYNE: NOW

"Your friend is crackers," Coyne said reversing out of the parking spot, shifting gears, and turning left at the sign for Newgrange.

"Mildred is not my friend. She's the mother of Kitty's friend, so I'm connected to her by osmosis. Ben is awesome, Mildred not so much. The fact she's with your father, I'll be hearing about it for years. I got a private tour of Dun Laoghaire by a Sir." Annie rolled down the window, the salt breeze blowing her hair."Speaking of private tours, let's hear yours."

"Since 1852, we've kept records of my immediate family. Not to brag, but before that time we're actually related to the Knight'sTemplar, around the 1300s when they came to Ireland and were imprisoned."

"Wow, wait until Mildred hears!" Annie shot him a sideways smile.

"Promise me I won't be there when you tell her." He grinned, then continued. "So, my great-great-great-grandparents were the ones who created our dynasty. Donal actually bought up land from landowners leaving for America, and get this, decided to plant potatoes."

"So, the country was devastated by the potato crop and your relative decided to harvest potatoes."Annie laughed. "See, my problem is I'd never have the foresight to do that."

"Well, it was a different variety and so he prospered. His son William is my great-great-grandfather. He met his bride Elizabeth when she flung horse manure at him. At their wedding, she gave him a flask with a sketch of horse manure on it."

Annie burst out laughing. "That's quite the story for the wedding reception. Go on. I can't wait to hear about the rest of the clan."

"William had a son named Alfred and Alfred married Betsy, no manure story, but they were high society. They had a son Coyne, who wanted nothing to do with the trappings, but try telling them."

"So, you're rich?" Annie giggled. "Yet, you drive a cab?"

"I help out at the castle when I can. All about customer service. Don't want to get a one-star rating on Yelp."

"We'll have to see." She smiled, smitten.

He pulled into the carpark at Newgrange and after they climbed out of the car, beeped it locked. Coyne slipped his hand to hers and Annie squeezed it.

"Are you going to tell me the history of Newgrange?" Coyne purchased their tickets from inside the tourist centre, and hopped on a shuttle bus. With the tip of his hat, the driver crossed a small bridge, then stopped in front of Newgrange. They exited the bus and proceeded to walk along the path.

The smell of deep rich soil, moss interspersed with iron from the rocks, hit Annie when she entered the cavern.

"It smells so natural here. If someone could package this smell, they would be rich."Annie sighed.

"Is that something you'd be interested in?" Coyne asked, pulling her along the corridor into a section away from the tourists.

"During the beginning of Covid, I worked at home and tampered around with lotions. It was kind of a hobby." Annie shrugged. "It didn't amount to anything."

"So far!" Coyne smiled.

"Pish tosh. Let me hear the details about Newgrange."Annie ran her hand along the rocks.

"Yes, mamam!" He pointed out the carvings on the rocks. "These spirals,if you notice, go counterclockwise toward the middle of the rock, then clockwise on the other side. Up here…" He reached up and showed her. "…the markings are like 'W's. Are you impressed? You will be when I tell you Newgrange was built over five thousand years ago, long before Stonehenge, and weighs more than two thousand tons."

"How did they get the stones here?"

"Simple farmers built this and took about four hundred people almost thirty years to build. The stones were left by the ice age." His chest puffed with pride, proud of his heritage."

"I don't think they were simple farmers," Annie crowed. "What did they use it for?"

"It was originally thought to be just a passage tomb, but now it's classified as an Ancient Temple. They had the ingenuity to line it up so it accentuated the sun during the winter solstice. It's quite a sight to see."

"I'd like to see it one day, the winter solstice," Annie said, "but was that the only time it was used?"

"It seemed to be used as a burial site for royalty. Archaeologists were able to extract DNA from a bone, and found the fellow's parents were very closely related, indicating royal lineage."

"Is that what you meant by a passage tomb? Was it like a cemetery of sorts?" Annie asked, engrossed in his story.

"Yes, cows used to graze on top of the mound, and laborers searching for rocks were the ones who located the massive stone doors and the hidden history inside."

They climbed back on board the bus, returning to the visitor's centre. They strolled to the end of the walkway, entering into a gift shop. Coyne stopped at the counter and purchased a fridge magnet.

"Here's a little something to remind you of your visit here today."

"Coyne, I enjoyed myself. Thank you for the tour. What's next on the agenda?" Annie asked.

"Well, I can give you a tour of Killiney Hill but like the name, there's a lot of hills to climb. So maybe we should leave it until tomorrow."

"Sure," Annie said, disappointment filling her tone.

"However, in about an hour, there is a concert in the People's Park. It's called The Ukulele Hooley, if you'd be interested in hearing it?" Coyne asked as they walked back to the carpark.

"Hooley, let's go to a hooley."

Chapter 35

KITTY: NOW

"Hey, Flossy, is it possible to get the key to my room? Mom is out with Coyne and she has the key." I asked. Ben leaned against the counter, checking out his phone.

"Sure, of course. Your mom and Coyne make a cute couple. It's good to see him smiling again after all the heartbreak he's had." Flossy handed over the key, eyeing Ben. "Who's your friend?"

Ben held out his hand. "I'm Big Ben from Vegas. I always wanted to say that!"

"Oh, right, Mildred's son." Flossy smiled. "Your mom is quite the character. Is it true she always wears a hat? I wasn't here when you guys checked in."

"That she does. She does like her hats." Ben smiled. "But what did you mean about Coyne having heartbreak."

"I'm not one to gossip about the boss, best let him tell you," Flossy said.

Kitty and Ben headed up the stairs, stopping at the door to her room. Holding the door open, she allowed Ben in first to get the full effect of the room.

"Holy crap, your room is so much nicer than ours. Want to trade?" Ben asked, spread-eagle on the bed. "I could get used to this."

"Don't get too comfy, this isn't your room. Mom is sharing with me, remember? That's if she gets back from her date with Coyne."

"What's with this Coyne guy? What heartbreak did he have?" He sighed so deeply, he rustled the pillowcase. "Speaking of heartbreak, what are the odds Finn would be here?"

"You need to go and talk to him. There could be a simple explanation as to why he ghosted you," I said, trying to be helpful, but also wanting my bed back. I so desired a nap.

"There's no excuse for ghosting anyone, especially me. A simple call or text would have sufficed. I'm not high maintenance," seeing her glance. "What? I'm not. I just like to be treated with respect. Is that too much to ask for?" Ben sighed again. "Did you hear some noises over in the corner? Do you think it's mice?"

"No, don't get me thinking about mice again. You need to talk to Finn. He seems like a decent guy. He calls me Harvard and named the two lambs Harvard and Yale. He went to Yale."

Ben flopped over on his stomach. "Great, a hot Yale vet who ghosted me. I'm useless."

Thankfully, a knock at the door interrupted his moaning. I went to open it, glad for any reprise not to have to listen to another Ben saga.

"Ben, I need to explain," Finn stood at the door, a large bouquet in hand.

"Sorry, I don't have anything to say to you. You only get one chance to ignore Ben and Ben isn't a doormat."

"Ben, quit talking to yourself in the first person. It's really annoying," I chastened him. "Listen to Finn.

He must have a good excuse for loving and leaving you in Vegas. Right, Finn?"

"Right, Harvard. I do have a good excuse for an Irish goodbye." Finn handed the flowers through the open door, not venturing uninvited inside the room. "Do you mind if I come in? It's a little embarrassing standing here in the hallway."

"Fine, you can come in." Ben relented, waving him into the room with another sigh. "I don't know what you can say to make it okay."

"I got a text from Coyne. Sir Alfred was dying."

"Okay, wasn't expecting that."

Chapter 36

ELMVILLE: 2 YEARS AGO

"Coyne, the crack in the drywall is getting longer. I think I can measure it now with a meter stick," Aislyn said, cuddling up to her husband on the sofa, a plaid blanket over her legs, Blackie, their collie's head, over one thigh.

Elmville, hidden behind the bric-a-brac on the fireplace mantel, grimaced at the happy family life. His fists tightened, knuckles turning white. Anger perforated his being as he mocked the family in an annoying sing-song.

"You're going to die. You're going to die."

The stable door of Antswer Cottage slammed shut, the cottage walls vibrating as Elmville sucked in his breath, then began to blow for all he was worth. Damn these Tobins.

"Mom, Dad, I'm home," Sion yelled as she popped her head into the living area and went to stand by the large fireplace. "Did you guys see the clouds outside? They're green. It's brilliant. On the way back home, there were some yellow colored."

"How was your day, dear?" Aislyn asked as she sipped her tea and closed her book. "Any gossip from the charity shop?"

"When your family represents most of the citizens

in the town, no one wants to share any news in case it gets back to Dad or Sir Alfred." Sion pouted. "Did I get any post?"

"Yes, on the hall table." Aislyn sipped her now cold tea, the wind whistling outside.

"Mom, why didn't you tell me?" Sion stomped from the room. "You know I'm waiting for acceptance and you can't be bothered to tell me?"

"In my defense, you just got in the door." Aislyn sipped her tea, used to her daughter's tantrums.

The smoke from the fire reared down into the room as the wind howled. Immediately, heavy rain began to torment the cottage. Coyne rushed to the window to see their trees bent over as if bowing before the wind.

"Get under a doorframe!" Coyne ordered as hail herded down against the thatched roof.

"Dad, that's not going to do any good. We need to get somewhere safe," Sion's voice high and hysterical.

"Aislyn, come on." Coyne and Sion hid under the kitchen table. Blackie tucked in Sion's arms, her hands covering the dog's ears as best she could.

The cottage shook on its foundations. Aislyn ran to the table. In her haste, she tripped over a rug. The figurines from the fireplace flew in every direction. A particularly large leprechaun, a family heirloom from Aislyn's mother, hovered for a moment, before smashing onto Aislyn's head. She fell backward, her head making contact with the steel fireplace poker. With disregard for her own safety, Blackie ran out to help her mistress. Elmville held his breath, stopping the crisis and internal wind tunnel, so Blackie could survive.

"MOM!" Sion cried out as she and Coyne rushed

to Aislyn's side, but the poker through her forehead foretold all—they were too late.

Aislyn was dead and Elmville was dancing an Irish jig on the mantel.

Chapter 37

KITTY: NOW

"Flossy, is it true Coyne has booked out the entire dining hall for us?" I was flattered, or rather my mom should be. I hadn't seen my mom so happy since, well, forever. I admit, somewhat grudgingly, it was nice to see, okay. I would love to find my twin flame, but the only flames I seem to be able to find are at the bonfires, which are fired up outside.

"Well, it doesn't take much when you own the Castle to request the dining hall. I've lost count as to how many dining rooms there are here, so not to worry the other guests aren't inconvenienced. I'll join you guys when you head outside to see the drone display."

"What drone display?" I asked, attempting to pull out a crease in my handkerchief hemmed dress. It was cut low, which accounted for the sweater I wore. Maybe in order to find my twin flame, I should be showing off the girls, but if that's all he was interested in, I wasn't.

"I would have thought in Vegas they would have them every night," Flossy stated, spreading out the brochures on the counter and adding more to the display holder.

"Did someone's kid do these pamphlets?" I asked, eyeing one of Dun Laoghaire. Again the picture was blurred, and the colors dull.

"I know, aren't they terrible? They've had the same ones since Hector was a pup." She grinned. "You would think with all the money Sir Alfred and Coyne have they would spend some of it on advertising. Don't get me started on the website. It originally came on a floppy disc."

"I have a degree in marketing, I could take a look at it. Who do I talk to about it?" I asked, giddy with joy. Maybe my degree would come in handy after all.

"To be honest, neither of them care. You have my permission to go to town on it," Flossy said, shaking my hand.

"No offense, but will they be okay with me doing it on your say so?" I asked, imagining myself in Vegas and a hotel clerk saying it was okay for me to work on their website. I don't think the owners would be too happy.

"Not to worry, I'm Sir Alfred's fiancée."

Chapter 38

DRURIE: NOW

Sixty-five-inch-high planters anchored the split staircase and provided excellent coverage for me to hide. I played peek-a-boo with an overflowing vine. If it didn't get out of my face and almost cause me to sneeze, I was going to rip it out by its roots.

Annie at the top of the stairs began descending the red carpet, her dress the color and texture of a dandelion seed. A locket around her neck caught the light, a prism of colors emanating. I sneaked a glance at Coyne, watching him gaze at her. I had witnessed how he had acted with Sion's mother and it was nowhere near the look he had while he observed her.

Annie was like a princess, her hand lightly holding the railing more for style than for balance. When she caught his eye, she smiled, the smile of a woman in love. As she reached the bottom of the steps, he ran up the remainder and wrapped his arm in hers, leaning forward to gently kiss her on the lips.

"You are too beautiful to behold," Coyne whispered, just for Annie and my ears.

"You are too sweet."

His suit was cut like a knife to his frame, the vest and tie matching in a starry blue pattern, setting off the color of his eyes in perfect harmony.

Coyne led her past the main dining room, through a hall bookended with columns and five-foot-high tables, anchoring stone planters, the colors as vibrant as a rainbow. Each table accentuated a different tinge. One table highlighted various shades of yellow, from paper-thin pale yellow, to golden, butter-colored, leading up to saffron, the boldest of the bold daffodil. Another table boasted blues, beginning with baby blue, leading to cyan to ultramarine blue, trumpeting to indigo. Each of the displays contained the same flower, marigolds. It was a sight to behold.

Like a mouse in a maze, I jumped from hidden spot to hidden spot, until I could find the mouse hole in the wall, unobserved by humans, it would appear to be a normal green leaf in a four-leaf clover, but when the light caught it at the right angle, one could tell the wallpaper didn't quite attach to the seam. That's when I ran inside and began to climb the elaborate tunneling system leading me to the dining hall. With the agility I didn't feel, but apparently my body was able to accomplish, I climbed through a cavity in the back of the century-old cuckoo clock. Scampering along the weaving carving of grapes, I settled into a crevice, worn thin by countless years of leprechaun spying to listen and learn.

From my vantage point, I couldn't see how many forks were laid beside the plates, but I could see the company situated around the table. I'm glad I was in a comfy spot, cause this was going to be a hoot. Tucked in beside my cubby hole, I located a dandelion leaf. Unfolding it, I recognized a smattering of herbs and seeds. Caraway mixed in with thyme and parsley. My stomach rumbled like an earthquake. So distracted with my brothers' issues, I couldn't remember the last time I'd eaten. I ripped off a portion of the dandelion leaf and cradled the seeds inside and masticated like I was a baseball player chewing tobacco, but I couldn't spit, I had to swallow. The wad was larger than I thought and a leprechaun's throat isn't large, so you guessed it. I got the hiccups.

And they were loud!

Chapter 39

ANNIE: NOW

"Thanks for pulling out the chair for me." She smiled up at Coyne as the grandfather clock rang with St. Michael's chimes. "I've never had a man do that for me before."

"Dad would have pulled it right out." Kitty laughed, settling herself across the table from her mom.

"Ben, are you really working for a famous singer?" Finn asked as he sat down beside Ben to the left of Kitty.

"I am, and she's so nice. We had a quick phone call and she's amazing. She asked all about me! You would think it would be all about her, but no, she wanted to know about me. I told her there wasn't much to tell."

Ben liked to draw out the conversation, as the table quieted. Sir Alfred and Mildred, the last to arrive, settled into their seats as waiters filled the water and wine glasses, then added baskets of warm bread and rolls to the table.

"Son, does that mean you're not working for that amadan? Sorry, that means arse in Irish," Sir Alfred asked, gulping down the wine like he was heading into the desert.

"No, I quit. I would have called it a day with Chas anyway, but Kitty told me how rude he was to Annie. I can't work for someone so mean to others." Ben placed the napkin on his lap and squeezed Finn's hand under the table.

"Remember how I drove him to the airport." Sir Alfred signaled for more wine. "Well, he had missed the Bitcoin convention and word got out he wanted to talk to me. Perfect opportunity one would think. He had me to himself all the way to the airport." Sir Alfred chuckled. "I do have the Blarney in me and like to talk. I drove and tried to make conversation, like to advise him on the latest Bitcoin Teekacoin is hot. Like a typical Crypto-Bro, he was so arrogant he said to me, 'I don't need advice from someone who drives a cab in this god-forsaken country.'"

Ben began to choke on his roll, his eyes watering as he attempted to catch his breath. He stood up. Finn jumped up out of his chair and slapped Ben on the back. The roll popped out, flying into the nearest floral arrangement.

"You saved my son's life." Mildred flew out of her seat, pushing back the chair, and it fell on its side. She thrust herself into Finn's arms.

"Mom, let him breathe, or I'll have to give him CPR." Ben caught Finn's eye, grinning as Finn mouthed—later.

Waiters swarmed the table adding plates piled high with mashed potatoes, cabbage, Irish stew, smoked salmon, black pudding, and more soda bread.

Coyne stood and tapped his wine glass with a knife.

"If I can have everyone's attention, though my speech will be anti-climactic after Ben's choking, but glad you're okay. I just wanted to thank the luck of the

Irish. Funny how life works out. Thanks to Mildred's misdiagnosis of Covid, Kitty and Annie came to our Emerald Isle. Otherwise, we never would have met. Everything happens for a reason. So, I'd like to raise a toast to our new friends and old friends. As we Irish like to say: May the hinges of our friendship never grow rusty. Cheers to our American friends."

Chapter 40

KITTY: NOW

"I've eaten so much I think I need to walk to Newgrange," I said to Ben, who was making goo-goo eyes at Finn.

"Ben, Finn, shift over. I want to sit beside Kitty," Flossy said, shoving Ben at his shoulder in an attempt to get him to move.

"Boy, she sure is bossy. I bet you were called Bossy Flossy at school." Ben laughed as he did as she asked.

"I forgot to ask Finn how Harvard and Yale are?" I asked, glad I wasn't the odd person out at the table.

"Harvard is asking about Harvard." Finn smiled as he held Ben's hand.

"Wait, why does he call you Harvard? You never went to Harvard?" Ben always was the fun ruiner.

"My mom bought me a sweatshirt with Harvard on it and Finn assumed I went there." I took pleasure in the look on Finn's face.

"At least the lamb Yale isn't a fraud." Finn made a comical face and stuck his tongue out at me.

"Quit hogging Kitty." Flossy turned her back to them and faced me. "So, I talked to Sir Alfred." She gave an exaggerated wave across the table to him before continuing. "He's happy for you to work on updating the website and brochures." She whispered, "It's so ancient we can't even accept payment for bookings. The other local hotels are killing us. The only thing we have going for us is we're a castle."

I hugged Flossy. "Thank you so much for organizing this. I'll get started on it right away. I'll take pictures of the area tomorrow." I hugged her again. "This is so much better than a date." I waved my hand around the table. "Look at how everyone is mated up."

Sir Alfred was entranced by something Mildred was saying, Mom and Coyne were off in their own world, and Ben and Finn were discussing the merits of *Kinky Boots*, The Musical.

"Doesn't it bother you Sir Alfred is so attentive to Mildred? He's your fiancé and not paying you any attention," I spit out the words, offended on her behalf.

"I was just joshing with you. He tells people at the counter I'm his fiancée when he doesn't want to be bothered with rude people." Flossy laughed. "Didn't you think he was a little too old for me? You Americans!" One of the waiters, about twenty-five, with hair redder than Prince Harry's squeezed her shoulder as he passed. "Colm's my boyfriend, and he's also doing the drone display. He's just helping me out tonight, we were shorthanded. He's a marine engineer." Flossy's eyes followed him around the room. "I know, I had no idea it was a career. On the first date I asked him how there could be trains under the ocean to which he replied have I never heard of the Chunnel. Which of course has nothing to do with what he does. I clicked with his sense of humor and the rest is history."

"Excuse me a sec." I put my napkin on the seat of my chair. I waited until Colm placed the food tray on the portable table, then asked my questions. I could see why Flossy was in love with him. He was mega cute and so patient with my questions. Plus he was the type of person who, when you spoke, you felt like you were the only person in the room. He made you feel special. I wonder if he had a brother.

I headed back to my chair and the hated look of Flossy.

"Are all Americans like you?" Flossy asked, her teeth clenched, spitting out her words.

"What do you mean?" I asked, still wrapping my head around what Colm said and how I could do as he suggested while keeping my friendship with Flossy.

"Moving in on Colm as soon as I told you he was my boyfriend. That's a shite move even for an American, but especially from someone I thought was my friend."

"I am your friend." I couldn't explain which was even worse.

Coyne stood up again and tapped his glass. "Everyone finished the spectacular meal? Let's have a round of applause for the kitchen staff and our master organizer Flossy, my father's fiancée. Sorry, Mildred, inside joke. No need to kill my father, at least not yet. Anyway, if we could wander outside to the bonfire, Colm has something to show us and I think we'll all be in awe."

Chapter 41

DRURIE: NOW

I scampered away from my hiding spot, reversing the course I had taken. I grabbed the remainder of the herbs and seeds, eating them slowly. Swinging amongst the boards, I felt like a monkey in the zoo. One-handed, I grabbed the handholds, careful not to get slivers from the wood. Thick cobwebs connected the corner of beams, the lace artwork produced by my friend Jasmine. Even in the hidden walls, she managed to entice ants, bugs, and even a bee into her web. She was one talented anachnid.

I reached the outside before the humans, wiping the cloying dust from my vest. They were a slow lot, reminding me of sloths, staggering along the cobblestone walkway. Each of them moaning and rubbing their stomachs to varying degrees.

Lawn chairs were set up in a circle around a firepit, and plaid blankets in a variety of tartans were flung over the chair backs. Trays balanced on tables filled with coffee urns, teapots, cups, in addition to the ingredients to roast marshmallows.

I took refuge in the branches of the yew trees, which formed the maze. Oh, fiddle sticks. One of the herbs I ate doesn't agree with me. My intestines weren't happy and I couldn't hold it in. I had to release.

"Do you mind changing chairs?" Mildred asked Sir Alfred. "There's something really smelly here and I think I'm going to be sick to my stomach."

"Of course, dearest. Anything for you." Sir Alfred shifted chairs. "I don't smell anything but I am more adjusted to the odd odors here. Any better, dearest?"

"Perfect, thank you." Mildred adjusted the blanket back over her legs and tilted her hat to the correct angle before accepting a cup of tea from Sir Alfred.

"This is so exciting. Colm has worked so hard on this display, I'm nervous for him." Flossy checked out the night sky. "At least the weather is cooperating. I was afraid it was going to rain. It's really brilliant. He uses small UAVs. They are equipped with LED lights and he times them with music."

On cue, the instrumental strings of "Irish Eyes are Smiling" began and the drones danced like lightning bugs in the sky. Hit song followed hit song as the humans watched the lights in the night sky. I attempted to get my mind off my stomach issues, but the gas was bubbling out of me like I was a volcano about to erupt.

"I smell it now too!" Sir Alfred admitted to Mildred as I tried to hold it in, but obviously unsuccessfully."

My bowel issues were forgotten as everyone's attention focused on the heavens.

The drones changed from a butterfly into a leprechaun, then twisted into a four-leaf clover. Gasps filled the air, as a word was written inside each of the clovers.

Gasps were replaced with a universal intake of breath and I don't think it had anything to do with my gas. Inside each of the clover leaves were the words

"Will You Marry Me?"

Mildred looked at Sir Alfred, Annie looked at Coyne, Ben looked at Finn, and Kitty looked at all three couples.

Coyne looked uncomfortable, Sir Alfred looked more uncomfortable, Finn looked even more uncomfortable, and Kitty looked at all three.

A new display of drones lit up under the clover and flashed like a disco ball. Flossy appeared, the drone so detailed it looked like a photo.

Colm came out from behind the computer, knelt in front of Flossy, and held out a ring as the clover hovered over their heads.

"Oh my god, yes, yes, yes." Colm slid the ring onto Flossy's finger as the crowd clapped and cheered.

I let out the breath I too had been holding, releasing the build-up of methane. I knew how to clear the area, as the drones forgotten, the humans held their noses and rushed inside.

"Congratulations, Flossy. Your ring is beautiful. Colm only talked about you and I was asking him questions about a project I'm working on."

"Sorry to be a shite. He was stressed and I thought he was going to break up with me. Thanks, Kitty, now you'll have an excuse to come back to Ireland. For the wedding." Flossy glowed brighter than the moon and drones, her ring catching the glow from the fire, beautifying her ring even more.

"I'd love to attend the wedding. I know someone I can borrow a hat from. I'm sure Mildred will help me out."

"Heck no, you're in the wedding party. So, you're going to have to come over earlier and stay longer,"

Flossy insisted.

I yawned and farted, but luckily the girls were too busy checking their phones for wedding dresses to notice me as I scurried across the cobblestones toward the castle.

"Did you see that?" Kitty asked. "I could have sworn I saw a leprechaun. He looked a little like the one I saw before my accident in Vegas."

"Oh yeah, it's a common occurrence, especially when you've had too much to drink. Come on, let's go and find my fiancé." Flossy locked her arm through Kitty's and they headed inside.

I was ticked off. Imagine the consensus leprechauns are only to be seen if you've been drinking. I'd show these humans a thing or two. Just wait until tomorrow at Newgrange. Elmville and I would show them a thing or two. Yep, all would be forgotten as Elmville and I had a common enemy. The enemy of my enemy is my friend.

Chapter 42

ANNIE: NOW

"Don't wait up for your mom," Coyne said to Kitty as he led her up the staircase. As they passed the room she shared with Kitty, she stopped.

"Just a second. I'm sorry but I have to gather my lotions and toothbrush. I have a routine and I can't break it."

He waited in the hallway as she rushed into the room and into the bathroom where she swiped her lotions and toothbrush into her Vegas or Bust make-up bag.

"Ready." She slid her hand into Coyne's, and walking on cloud nine, her feet barely touching the ground, they stopped at a set of double doors and walked into Coyne's suite.

"Wow, I thought our room was impressive," Annie announced. The room was a combination of a sitting room and a separate bedroom, the large bed she could see from the open door. A fireplace warmed the room, flanked by leather sofas and antique tables. Lampshades decorated with gold fringe; the lights dimmed.

Coyne poured glasses of champagne and handed one to Annie before taking one for himself.

"Did I tell you how beautiful you looked tonight?" Coyne raised his glass to her.

"Thank you. It was fun to get dressed up and go to a fancy dinner." Annie sipped her drink, then placed it back on the table, stepping closer to Coyne. "Thank you for…"

Annie couldn't finish her words before Coyne fingered her locket and she lost her train of thought. Her skin heated at his touch. He tucked her hair behind her ear, trailing his finger back down to the necklace, then down to her cleavage. His touch feather-light.

"I don't want to kill the mood but I haven't been with anyone since I lost Sion's mother." Coyne bit his lip, fearing he did just that.

"I haven't been with anyone since Kitty's father left me. He made me feel I wasn't important enough for anyone else to want me," Annie admitted, pouring more champagne into her glass and gulping it down.

"What a pair we are." Coyne stood by the fire, then in two strides was back beside Annie. "Your ex was an eejit. His name wasn't Chas, was it?" Coyne lowered his eyes to her mouth, took her in his arms, wrapping his hand around the back of her neck, and pulled her closer, kissing her. Annie kissed back, their tongues dancing.

"There's a bed in the other room," Coyne stated the obvious, staring at her adoringly.

"I think we should check it out, but first, I need you to do something for me."

"Anything, my love. I would do anything for you." Coyne's thumb caressed the vein on the inside of her wrist.

Annie turned her back to Coyne and lifted her hair.

"I want you to remember our last night together before I have to leave tomorrow night. I need you to unzip this dress. It's way too confining for what I have in mind."

Chapter 43

KITTY: NOW

"I was playing around with different scenarios." She moved her laptop across the sign-in desk, for Flossy.

Flossy chugged down half a bottle of water, while Kitty pushed buttons.

"I have a wedding dress I have to fit into. I'm only drinking water from now until the wedding. And no, we haven't set a date, so I should be a size zero by the time it comes." Flossy grinned. "I'll be so waterlogged, Colm won't recognize me."

"You're crazy, you do know that, right?" Kitty shifted the laptop and angled the screen to avoid the glare from lamps positioned on the counter. "So, I was thinking of something along these lines."

The screen showed a picture of the castle, the curser instead of an arrow, was a small leprechaun. "When you move the leprechaun around, like for example here, it opens up the lobby and there are 360-degree pictures." I shifted the mouse. "Okay, then if you click on the computer on the counter, it shows booking details. The calendar pops up and specials."

"How do they know where to click?" Flossy asked, moving her ring around so it caught the lights, the colors radiating off the diamond centered between two

Celtic knots.

"The leprechaun changes color." Kitty bragged, "That especially took time, but I'm really happy with the result. I was going from memory as to what he looked like. This little guy is like the one I saw before my accident in Vegas."

"You've seen Elmville?" Flossy asked.

Kitty paused. "Sorry, who's Elmville?"

"That, my friend, is Elmville." Flossy pointed to the curser. "Elmville is the leprechaun known in the area for hating the Tobins and has caused pain and suffering through the centuries."

"It wasn't my imagination?" I felt nauseous, swallowing bile so I didn't throw up. "Are you telling me this thing actually exists?"

"Yep, though he and his brother Drurie won't appreciate the fact you called them a thing. They hate each other, but you can't talk bad about them. Then they gang up together on us and they can be vicious, especially Elmville. Legend has it his coin was lost or stolen, depending on who is telling the story. The coin balances a leprechaun's yin and yang and without it, Elmville is just evil."

Obviously, I had the solution. "Why not just give the coin back to him?"

"The conditions have to be right. It has to be handed back to the place where it was originally lost. Of course, over the centuries, the legend has grown by expeditious proportions, so no one knows where it originally was lost. But who cares about that? What else do you have to show me?" Flossy asked, again fingering her ring like a worry stone.

"This is why I was asking Colm's advice." I

clicked another tab and on the screen was the doll house, the replica of the castle. "With this one, it begins with stars, then with Colm's help, they morph like the drones did into different shapes." In front of our eyes, the UAVs became shamrocks, and inside the clovers were words, bookings, local sights, fun, food. The sound of fiddles filled the air, soaking the room with the song "Irish Eyes Are Smiling."

"I hope you don't mind I used Colm's ideas, but this way, your proposal is immortalized. Also, I thought you could use pictures of your wedding to sell the prospect of using Castle Whitestone as a wedding venue." I didn't want to see her reaction, so I rushed on. "I'm going to head out today before Mom and I leave to take some local pictures, and when I get home, I can work on the brochures and website remotely and send the results to you." I paused to take a breath, slowly raising my eyes to gauge her thoughts.

"I hate you. Do you realize how awesome this looks?" Flossy squealed.

"Then why do you hate me?" I was never going to understand these Irish folks.

"Because I'm going to be so busy, I'll never see Colm." Flossy laughed. "What about if you shade the edges around the dollhouse so it looks fairy-ish? Do you think it would look too busy if we had the original picture from the first one you showed me and the drones from the second one?" Flossy bit her lip, tracing her finger along the screen to show me her intentions.

"Let me play around with it a bit and we'll see what I can come up with. But you like it?"

"Kitty, it looks awesome." The grandfather clock in the lobby chimed. "There are over seventy clocks in this castle, and this one is reminding us we'd better get you moving if you're going to get all this stuff done before you catch your plane."

"Right. Have you seen my mom this morning? She didn't come home at all last night and I wanted to touch base with her before I left. She spent the night with Coyne."

"I haven't but I'll pass on the message when I do see her. Don't be too long. You don't want to miss your plane."

Chapter 44

ANNIE: NOW

Annie caught sight of Coyne from the bathroom mirror, his lean torso uncovered by the sheet. The view of him caused her toes to curl in memory of the waves of pleasure he brought to her body last night. Impossible as it was to believe, she had felt herself dissolve at his finger-light touch. Reliving the night brought an ache with inner longing. How was she going to go back to Vegas when her heart and her orgasms were left in Dun Laoghaire?

Don't go there Don't ruin the remainder of the time you have left with him being all teary-eyed and moany.

She lined up her lotions, lathering them in order onto her face. She used the white buttery soft facecloth to wash her face as she felt arms wrap around her waist, butterfly kisses on her neck.

Coyne rested his head on her shoulder, eyeing the bottles and jars on the counter. "What are VeganVegas Lotions?"

"These are the lotions I was telling you about. I made them up during the height of Covid, but I'm not the type of person to hype myself up, so they didn't take off. Kitty was in one of her moods, so I didn't even ask her to design the packaging." She stopped. "I printed off a lot of stickers. I thought it was cute using the two V's in VeganVegas Lotions as legs but apparently, it's not politically correct in today's environment. I have a garage filled with boxes and cartons of them. I use them whenever I can. I don't want to waste them and throw them out. It would be like admitting I was a failure."

Coyne grabbed a towel from the rack and wrapped it around his torso before stepping around in front of her and picking up the closest jar.

He removed the lid and inhaled. "What does this one do? Comfrey Comfy?"

"The main ingredient is comfrey. It's good for muscle strains. This one here is to lessen bags and dark circles under your eyes. I tried to keep in line with what people do in Vegas. You know, late nights and early mornings. And too much dancing. Anyway, nothing ventured, etc."

"I think it's a great idea and I'm proud of you." He faced her in front of the mirror. "Now, I've got the day planned, but the dress you wore last night will be inappropriate for our adventure. Also, I won't be able to concentrate on driving if you're wearing it."

"I'll head back to my room and get packed up. Can you give me half an hour and I'll meet you downstairs?" Annie asked. "My urge is to whip off the towel but then we'd never get downstairs, not that that is a bad thing but I do want to pick up a few last-minute things."

"We have time for a quick towel whip-off." Coyne grabbed Annie, lifted her, and carried her back to the bed.

An hour later, her hair still wet from the shower,

her lotions reapplied, Annie headed down the stairs in her runners, jeans, and a light sweater, her neck adorned with the locket, her arm with the bracelet, her face glowing from the aftermath of great sex.

"Looks like someone is a tad flushed," Flossy teased Coyne who turned to watch Annie head downstairs. "What did you do to the poor woman? She sure doesn't look like the one who arrived here last week." Flossy chuckled, covering her ears with her hands and repeating lalalala. "I do not want to know. What are you kids up to today? Oh, by the way, Annie, Kitty said she was going out to take pictures for the website and she'd be back in time for the plane."

"Okay, thanks for passing on the message. We'll probably see her in town. Flossy, if I don't see you before I go, I just wanted to thank you for looking after us while we were here. You are awesome and a true representative of the Irish people."

"I think Coyne represented the Irish people better than I ever could but you'll be back. I don't think Coyne is going to let you get away."

Coyne picked a pen up off the counter and tossed it playfully at Flossy. "Hush you! Is there a must-see?"

Annie wrapped her arm in Coyne's. "I'm easy. Whatever you have planned is good for me. Time is a marching, let's get on."

"As the lady wishes." Flossy laughed, happy to see her boss so happy.

Chapter 45

DRURIE: NOW

I trudged through the walls of the castle, sliding between an ancient tapestry and the wall. I followed the markings I had made previous times, as I had no sense of direction in this part of the castle. A fork from the kitchen Elmville had borrowed leaned against a cement block. Even I laughed the first time I witnessed it. Yes, indeed, it was a fork in the road. I turned left, then right then another sharp left. Next, I had to squeeze through three darning needles placed in a triangle before coming up to a gold, yes gold, plated door with a crudely printed DO NOT ENTER. All of the e's were backward. Without knocking, as I heard him before I saw him. His snores were raising the bedcovers. I nudged my brother Elmville out of his hammock, the lace-like silk created by Jasmine sticking to the back of his knobby knees before they sprung back into their original position.

"Diaduit, brother. Time to rise and shine and wake the cobwebs out of your bones," I admonished my brother. He wasn't known for much but sleeping was his talent of choice. He could sleep for days. His nickname was Van Winkle Elmville.

"Let me sleep. I was up late last night and need my sleep. *Pogmothoin.*" Elmville crawled back into the sling before I grabbed the side and tossed him out.

"You need to get the coin back. I'm not going to go through any more centuries of being teased because my brother can't even hang onto his leprechaun coin. Enough is enough."

"You're such a dry shite." Elmville took my cap and tossed it onto the dusty floor of the hovel. Really, how immature, and here I was trying to help him. I had every intention of turning on my heels and leaving him in the mess he'd gotten himself. Though it still didn't solve my problem of having a noob for a brother, who would forget his round-toed shoes if they weren't permanently attached to his feet.

I sat perched on the edge of his hammock, rocking myself back and forth while I waited for him to pick some snacks out of the wall beams. Who knew what a feast awaited one in the walls of the castle? I preferred the food Flossy left out for me, though she liked to pretend I didn't exist, and to be honest, I too liked to play make-believe that she didn't exist either. What can I say? It worked for both of us.

Elmville coughed repeatedly. "That grasshopper went down the wrong way, but I'm good now."

We made our way back toward the tapestry at the back of the room, which held the dollhouse. We were walking single file, and I held up my hand like a traffic cop, stopping him in his tracks. Kitty was taking pictures of the dollhouse and I didn't want us to be a part of it. Though if we spun around quickly enough, we'd look like a blur or more like an orb. (Now you know the answer to those green orbs you see in your photos. You're welcome!)

Chapter 46

ANNIE: NOW

"Would you like to see Blarney Castle?" Coyne asked, settling Annie into the car and leaving the carpark of the castle. "It's about a three-hour drive."

"How about we skip it? You fill me in on the fun facts about Blarney and we relax and see the sights around the area. You are all I'd like to kiss." She leaned over and kissed his cheek.

"Sounds perfect, but I think we can improve on the kiss." Coyne cupped her chin with his hand, pulling her closer. His lips on hers as light as a feather, his tongue darting in and out teasingly."Or we could head back to the castle and spend the rest of the day in bed," Coyne suggested, raising his eyebrows.

"You do like to tempt me. No speeding tickets, but I think that's a good game plan." Once Coyne finished shifting gears, Annie took his hand, intertwining her fingers with his, their hands resting on her thigh, just below her sundress.

"You are the temptress." Coyne stroked her leg, goosebumps erupting on her skin. "Blarney is, of course, known for the Blarney Stone. Legend has it that if you kiss it, you will be given the gift of the gab. Apparently, there's a missing piece of the rock and it's at a university in America, but who knows." He continued to gently rub her leg.

"But why kissing? Not that I have anything against kissing." Annie lifted their hands and kissed his knuckles.

"Definitely you don't, and you are quite good at it." He grinned. "You witch, you're trying to get me sidetracked. Speaking of witches, the owner of the castle was approached by one. He was on his way to see the queen who was going to take away his land. The witch told him to kiss the first large rock he saw, so he did and the queen settled in his favor. So, he incorporated the stone into the castle. Another story was it was part of Jacob's pillow he slept on when he dreamed of the ladder reaching heaven, decorated with angels."

"Oh, I hope they are both true. Both are romantic, don't you agree? Though it couldn't have been too comfy sleeping on a stone pillow."

Coyne signaled a turn, then paralleled parked near the site before replying, "I guess it depends on who you're sharing the pillow with. You wanted to see Newgrange again, here we are for a quick tour, then we'll head back to the hotel."

"True, and yes, thank you. There's something about Newgrange that draws me to it." Annie unbuckled her seatbelt, pulled down the visor, and checked her hair in the mirror. She straightened the locket, fiddling with the clasp not quite catching. She fluffed her hair and then climbed out of the car. "Newgrange gets prettier and prettier every time I see it."

"You'll have to see it on the Winter Solstice. It's totally brilliant."

They headed up the hill toward the visitor center Bru na Boinne, where the architect mimicked the historical site with rounded walls, the same shade as the site. Annie glimpsed the long bridge crossing the River Boyne. Coyne held open the door for Annie and they headed inside to the air-conditioned building.

A man with a badge "Alex, the tour guide" voice boomed across the lobby. "The next tour begins in fifteen minutes. I suggest you use the washroom before we get started. Reminds me, I'll see you folks in a minute." Chuckling, his round belly jiggling, Alex headed toward the sign of a man with his legs crossed.

"Coyne, lad, is that you?" Alex's voice vibrated across the room. "Well, as I live and breathe. What brings you to us? Did this beautiful lass have anything to do with you visiting us?" Alex bowed at Annie. "Lass, I need to warn you, you need to be careful around this one."

"Too late for that, but please explain," Annie inquired, noting now that she needed to use the washroom before they headed out.

"You might be able to tell from my accent I'm Scottish. So, when I fell in love with my Bonnie and she wouldn't leave Ireland, I came here. Coyne was my first mate. Gave me my first job. Tours of the Castle."

"Then you promptly left me and came to Newgrange. That's the thanks you get for helping someone out. As the saying goes, find a friend brave and true, you screw him before he screws you." The belly laughter from the two men almost caused an avalanche from the free-standing flags.

"Don't listen to him. I help out gratis when the busy season starts up. The stories I could tell you about the castle…" Alex winked.

"About the castle or about Coyne?"

"Oh, Coyne stories are much more interesting. Can we catch up later? My inner workings aren't what they once were, and I don't want to be using the trees outside. Kind of lowers the tips, if you know what I mean. Especially if I have my back turned to the ladies."

"Oh goodness, I bet he's kissed the Blarney Stone." Annie chuckled.

"He gave tours there as well and he demonstrated for the visitors, so he's probably kissed it more than he should and that's the result. He was probably there the day we were here last."

Annie headed into the washroom, used the loo and the sink, then headed back to Coyne and the group waiting for Alex. Listening to the chit-chat of the others, Annie and Coyne wandered away.

"You certainly know a lot of different characters. From Jonob to Alex. Oh, the gift shop is open, and no one is in there yet. Let's go inside and check it out."

Rows of scarves were lined up on the top of a bureau, t-shirts hung on rows, some tilted to the sides as if pulled off gravity. Postcards, placemats, and mugs were stocked along glass shelves.

"There seems to be a lot more inventory than the last time we were here. Though I do love my fridge magnet," Annie mused, then jumped as a cowbell rang.

"Sorry, I should have warned you. Alex likes to pretend he's the town crier."

Gathering together his flock, Alex led them outside to the shuttle bus. Coyne and Annie managed to get two seats together and held hands while waiting for the others to board.

Alex did a tally and headcount. "We're just waiting for one slowpoke." Alex surveyed the parking lot in search of the wayward person. Checking his watch, he nodded to the driver. "Well, like our train system, we wait for no man or woman. Onward, Clive."

"Wait, wait, wait." Kitty came tearing across the carpark.

Alex, apparently used to the tardiness of Americans, shook his head. "Catch the next shuttle. It will leave in fifteen minutes."

"Wait, can you please make an exception? That's my daughter." Annie panicked.

"I should have known it would have something to do with you, Coyne." Clive stopped the bus and Kitty boarded.

"Thanks so much. I got caught up taking pictures of your beautiful country." Kitty smiled at Alex as she settled into her seat, turning to wave at Coyne and Annie.

"Sounds to me like you've been at the castle, kissing the Blarney Stone."

Chapter 47

DRURIE: NOW

We were tucked under the wheel well of the shuttle bus, a favorite place of ours. We might have smaller brains than humans, but when it came to getting a free ride, we had all the issues figured out.

Elmville had even hitched a ride on a flight to America, though he did admit he should have planned a little better. He was stuck beside one of the turbo fans. Between the noise and the wind, he was not a happy hitchhiker.

Elmville was spread eagle on the axle, while I resorted to the springs, so I wasn't feeling every bump.

The color drained from Elmville's face, and his body twitched. Spasms rocked through his body as he wrapped his legs around the metal to avoid falling off.

"Bro, what's up?" I left my comfy spot and climbed over to the axle. His body was shaking, reminding me of leaves during a massive windstorm. "Talk to me. What can I do to help?"

"Nothing, just let me be. I don't know what's happening. I think I'm dying." The tremors lessened as the bus came to a stop and we could see legs and feet walking away from the bus.

"Let's get out of here and head to the passage tomb," I ordered as we left our positions and slid down the tires to the gravel carpark.

Elmville, recovered from his shakes, was still a tad wobbly on his legs, but when I grabbed his arm to give him some balance, he shook me off. Stubborn he was, and full of flatulence. Good thing I had my hands free to plug my nose.

The annoying voice of the tour guide grated on me, no doubt from all the bagpiping. I tuned him out. I'd heard this particular speech so many times, I could have given it myself. Tales from a leprechaun, now *that* would sell tickets.

Chapter 48

COYNE: NOW

Exhaust coughed from the shuttle bus as it chugged its way up the hill, reminding Coyne of the train from a children's book.

Alex could peel an orange in his pocket he was so tight with money, and he didn't repair the bus until it was on its last wheels. It appeared to be today, as the bus stopped and began to roll back down the incline. Clive threw up the handbrake, stopping the bus.

"Okay, folks, we have a little bit of engine trouble, so we're just going to call in for some support and they will bring us another bus."

Groans erupted throughout the bus as one cocky jerk asked how long it would take.

"I left my fortune-telling equipment at home, lad, but we'll just have to sit tight." Alex remained calm under the pressure of the unhappy passengers.

"I want a refund," the same voice called out. "I didn't pay for this delay and I demand you correct it."

Coyne pivoted in his seat to see who was causing his friend such grief but couldn't see over the tall headrest.

"Mate, he's doing the best he can," Coyne stated, before turning back around.

"You Brits all stick together. Off with your heads,"

the voice yelled.

Everyone vacated the bus, and as the passengers filed past Coyne and Annie, Annie gasped.

The mouthy American was Chas.

Chapter 49

KITTY: NOW

After an hour's wait, we made it to Newgrange. Mom and I ignored Chas. I was so not getting drawn into his drama.

I slung one strap of my backpack over my shoulder, and with my phone in hand, set on camera mode, I began to record. Sheep grazing down the hill from the passage tomb, a slight dew on the ground, while clouds danced across the sky.

Mom and Coyne were lost in their own world as I snapped photos. I squeezed the picture on my phone to maximize their heads and lose most of the background. Mom's face was glowing, but her necklace didn't clasp and she would lose it. They headed around the back of Newgrange, past the kerbstones, each with different carvings as I rushed to catch them.

Before I could reach them, a commotion erupted from their direction. The others on the tour were inside with Alex, but from where I stood, I could smell the odor reminiscent of the bonfire night.

I ran around the side, stopping short.

"Elmville, stop!" I bellowed as I took in a leprechaun, his legs on either side of my mother's neck, ripping off the locket.

He twisted his body at my voice as he convulsed.

The necklace forgotten, he fell to the ground, lying still.

Another leprechaun, dressed in red, hurried to his side, kneeling. All attempts to remain hidden were forgotten in his concern.

"Please, you must do something. He's my brother." His face streaked with tears, he wiped his dripping nose on the back of the sleeve of his waistcoat.

Reaching into my backpack, I found some of Mom's lotions and began to spread them over his clothes, knowing the cream would seep through onto his skin. It was a good five minutes before he stirred. He tried to sit up, only to fall back again.

Mom and Coyne stood further back. Mom obviously did not want to get too close to the action in case Elmville attempted thievery again.

"How do you know its name?" Mom asked, redness creeping up her neck from the tugging.

"He's the one I saw when I had my accident and Flossy filled me in on his name when she saw the work I did on the website. Mom, I told you I wasn't on drugs." I continued to massage the cream into his clothes as he began to move about, flexing one leg and then the other.

"You carry around my lotions?" Mom asked, eyeing the jars. "I thought you believed it was all a waste of time and money."

"No, Mom, it's good stuff. I keep it in my backpack. I've gone through lots of it, though maybe we should work on updating the packaging. VeganVegas and two showgirl legs?"

"If I win the lottery, we'll see." Mom reached down and patted me on the head, and for once, I didn't mind.

Propped up by his brother, Elmville sheepishly said, "I'm sorry if I hurt your neck. You don't know how many centuries I've been hunting for my coin. I overreacted."

"What coin? You were trying to steal my locket?" Mom used her mom's voice and I could tell Elmville wasn't used to being spoken to with that tone.

"Look inside the locket," Elmville's brother suggested.

Mom lifted her hair as Coyne unclasped the locket, redoing it before handing it back to Mom. When she opened it, the leprechaun coin fell to the ground, inches from Elmville's hand.

He didn't reach for it, though his fingers stretched in the direction.

"What's so important?" Mom asked, not moving to retrieve it.

Elmville's brother spoke. "If I may. A leprechaun needs his coin to balance his yin and yang. Without a coin, he is evil. No offense, brother. Over the centuries, beyond his control, he's had a vendetta against the Tobins. All in the attempt to get his coin returned."

"Then definitely, you must have it back," Mom insisted.

Coyne, silent until now, directed his words toward Elmville. "Did you have anything to do with the tornado that killed my wife?"

"I'm sorry. It was like I was possessed. I couldn't help myself. I will do penance for the rest of my life, which will be a very long time. I wish there was something I could do or say to bring her back," Elmville stated, the words heartfelt.

"I would happily strangle you, but nothing will

bring her back and I've moved on. I could never understand how the victim's family in a courtroom could not jump over the rails and kill the person who took their loved ones away, but I can now." Coyne glanced over at Annie and saw his future, while his past remained where it belonged.

"Will the curse be removed now? Will no further harm come to my family?" Coyne asked the brother, the wound still too raw to talk to Elmville.

"Yes, definitely, and my name is Drurie."

"I'm not a Tobin, so why the car accident in Las Vegas? But Fred, the guy who rescued me, was a Tobin." I screwed the lid onto the lotion jar and handed it to Drurie. "In case you need more tonight."

"Sorry about that. It was just a coincidence Fred's last name is Tobin. Short men are quite popular in Vegas and I got a little carried away with the drinks and the women." He paused and snorted in his defense."I wanted to see Area 51."

"What's everyone doing back here? The tour is finished and we're heading back on the bus," Alex said. "Sometimes this tour is like herding sheep. Everyone just goes off on their own."

Mom picked up the coin and handed it to Elmville. "I'm sorry you had to go through so much to get it back. It belongs to you, so enjoy." She threaded her arm through Coyne's as they headed back to the shuttle bus.

"Kitty, come on, or we're going to miss our plane," Mom yelled across the carpark, turning the heads of everyone who heard her.

"Too late for that, Mom. It left half an hour ago."

Chas grimaced. "Seems you never could get your dates and timing right. Wondering, though, if you'd like to come and work for me once you get back. If you ever get back. I need an assistant, and while your calendar skills are dismal, I could use someone to scrape the shite off my shoes."

Coyne walked over to Chas, drew back his arm, and punched him in the nose. Without rubbing the soreness out of his knuckles, Coyne wiped the blood from his hand and turned to Kitty. "Would you have some more of your mom's lotion?"

Wordlessly, she handed it to him at the same time Drurie handed some to him, as well.

"Well done, mate," Drurie added. "You don't know how long I wanted to do that!"

"I'll sue you," Chas spat, while holding his nose as if it would fall off his face.

"I think in order to sue, you need witnesses and I can attest no one here saw a thing." Annie and Kitty nodded, as did Drurie and Elmville. Elmville climbed on one of the kerbstones, and high-fived Coyne.

"I guess I'll be checking flights when we get back to the castle." Annie rifled through her phone.

"Don't worry. We'll get it all sorted. Just need to make a phone call," Coyne said, digging out his phone as well and typing feverously.

Chapter 50

KITTY: NOW

The lobby was empty, except for Chas, who sat alone in one of the chair groupings, reading an upside-down newspaper.

"So I guess this is goodbye?" I walked around behind the counter to hug Flossy. "Thank you for everything."

"I should be thanking you. Look at the desk helpers you found for me." Both grimaced at the antics of Drurie and Elmville. Like divas, they had insisted on being front and center at the castle. Alex was a little perturbed when he found out his tours were replaced, given by actual leprechauns. Business was booming. The doll house had been moved beside the counter and the leprechauns bounded through the rooms to the delight of the children and adults alike. With the use of a padded basket, lined with tartan, the brothers would give a personalized tour, which included the hidden staircases used by humans in the olden days. Some things needed to be kept secret, so of course, their own hiding spots were never revealed.

"I'm going to revamp the website some more and when Newgrange saw what we did with this website, they asked me to make theirs more interactive. Looks like I have another job lined up, so I'll be heading back."

Finn and Ben strolled toward the counter as Coyne and Annie joined the group.

"Hope there's room on the plane for one more. Finn is heading over. He's going to be working for Vets without Borders, based in Vegas."

"How will that work with your new position with our favorite singer Cacti?" I asked, afraid of the answer.

"Perfect. She's doing a residency and after that, maybe we'll head back to the Emerald Isle." Ben kissed Finn on the mouth, oblivious to his mother walking into the room with Sir Alfred at her side.

"Ben, you don't have to keep thanking him for saving your life." Mildred adjusted her tiara. She'd forgone the hats once she discovered Sir Alfred was an actual Sir and had met King Charles, even though it wasn't an overly popular meeting in Ireland. To an American, it was the height of poshness.

"I'm glad everyone is here. I have some news." Sir Alfred rallied the group around him. "I don't know if you remember, Annie, when we were in the Leprechaun's Door at Trivia Night?"

Annie nodded.

"You handed me some pound notes to buy us a round. Well, I bought the round and used your money to purchase some Teekacoin. It's the latest online currency. I tried to explain it to you, but with the noise and the googly eyes you were making at my son, I just went ahead and did it."

"Sure! But it's your fault—your son is pretty hard to ignore."

"Yes, well, it's in our genes." Sir Alfred squeezed Mildred's arm. She glanced at Ben.

"Anyway, the money ballooned, and I reinvested it. Again it ballooned, and I had a feeling and cashed it in. Go with your gut, I always say." He handed Annie a check.

"Sir Alfred, this is for five hundred thousand pounds."Annie leaned toward Coyne, afraid she would faint.

"I think I'm entitled to some of that money." Chas jumped up from the chair, barging into the group.

"In what universe do you think you deserve a portion of that money?" Coyne asked, his fist raised as Annie cupped her hand in his to lower it.

"Stop right there, young man," Sir Alfred ordered. "I drove you to the airport, and you didn't want to hear anything I had to say. As I recall, you said I was a lowly cab driver, so there's a lesson for you. Often a person's mouth broke his nose."

Chas opened his mouth, then thought twice about it as he witnessed everyone including the leprechauns, form a circle around Annie and the check.

"Fine, you haven't heard the last from me. I'll see you all shortly at the airport." His words echoed a menacing threat.

"I doubt that." Coyne laughed as he saw the surprise on Annie's face.

"Just wait, my darling." Coyne kissed her forehead and rolled her luggage out of the lobby, her hand clutching the check, refusing to allow it out of her sight.

Chapter 51

ANNIE: NOW

Annie reached into her purse and removed the gift-wrapped item for Coyne as they headed into the shuttle bus for the airport.

"Alex, do you guarantee we'll get to the airport in time?" Annie teased.

"I don't think it matters, but yes, it's been completely rehauled. She's as fresh as a newborn and ready for another twenty years." He used his sleeve to wipe fingerprints off the railing.

Annie settled into her seat beside Coyne and handed him the present. "Thank you for a wonderful holiday. I love it's not goodbye when you're staying with us for the foreseeable future."

"The benefits of having an import/export business are I can travel at any time." Coyne began to unwrap the present. "You don't need to get me anything. You are enough."

"I saw this in the charity shop and Sion wrapped it up for me on the sly." Annie suddenly became nervous he wouldn't like it. She didn't know him all that well when she'd purchased it. Maybe he didn't use a flask.

Tears welled up in Coyne's eyes as he removed the paper his daughter had so carefully covered it. "How did you know?"

"Know what?"

"This was my great-great-grandfather William's," Coyne stated. "I thought it was lost forever in the tornado where Sion's mother was lost to us. This is further confirmation to me we are meant to be together."

The shuttle bus pulled through the side gate at the airport, and after passports were all checked and confirmed, they were waved through.

"Are we lost?" Annie asked as the bus drove them through into an airplane hangar.

"Definitely not. I called in a favor and we're flying on this beauty."

"Are you kidding me?" Kitty asked. "Are you telling me I flew steerage on the way here and now private on the way home?"

"Looks that way, dear," Annie chimed in.

Clive removed their baggage from the underbelly of the bus and put it in the cargo area of the plane. A uniformed flight attendant, straight from the society pages, stood at the bottom of the metal stairs, while another stood at the top.

Mildred stopped to discuss the hats they wore as Sir Alfred pulled her along, smiling apologetically.

Annie and Coyne sat on the leather bench seats, while the others found seats elsewhere on the plane. As they settled in, the flight attendant dispensed drinks of champagne and orange juice.

"Whose plane is this?" Annie whispered as she buckled up her seatbelt.

"Let's just say important people don't call my dad a cab driver, and they listen when he talks." Coyne laughed at the look of disbelief on her face.

The pilot's voice came over the loudspeaker. "Just waiting on one bloke and then we're ready to take off."

"God, I hope it's not Chas," Annie moaned.

"He wouldn't get past security." Coyne slung his arm around her shoulders as he sipped the cocktail.

Chapter 52

KITTY: NOW

"Mom, I've been working on some new logos for the lotions. What do you think?" I handed over the laptop and watched Mom scroll through the ideas. My favorite was Drurie and Elmville on their backs, their legs spread in a V-formation, representing each of the Vs in VeganVegas. Mom was adamant about keeping the name.

"I've been in talks, as well. We're going to showcase them in the castle as well as various tourist attractions in Newgrange," Coyne added. "I think the healing powers will be an excellent tie-in with Newgrange."

"If it can cure a leprechaun, it will get rid of your aches and pains," I suggested. "Maybe need to shorten it a bit. I'll work on it."

"Is this seat taken?"

"No, go ahead." I was entranced with my ideas and waved the man to the seat beside me. "Mom, maybe something like 'It's not a sin to use our cream.'"

"I like that," the male answered.

"Thanks." I finally looked up and matched the face to the voice. The wavy cocoa brown hair offset indigo-colored eyes. His physique showed he spent time at the gym and not just to sit on the equipment. "Where do I know you from?"

"I was in *People* magazine last month." He wasn't bragging, just stating it as fact, as he folded his six-foot frame into the seat.

I ignored Ben's waving like a flag on Memorial Day weekend.

"No, it's not that. Wait, did your grandmother fly to Ireland a while ago?" When he nodded, I continued. "I sat beside her in steerage and she showed me your picture. She sure is proud of you."

"My grandmother doesn't like to take anything from me. So, she flies economy, but if women like you are flying economy, maybe I'll sell my plane."

"That would be a shame," I said, looking around the interior as the flight attendant approached with hot towels and trays of fresh fruit.

"By the way, I'm Kitty and that's my mom and her boyfriend, Coyne."

"Nice to meet you, Kitty. You were helping your mom with a logo. I'm in need of a head of marketing. Can you show me some of your work?"

"Sure. What kind of company is it to give me an idea?"

"I'm Prince Cloverdale, and my company has the license on leprechauns. My lineage goes way back."

Epilogue

Las Vegas is the city of opportunity if you know how to use it properly. Some did, like Annie, who used the money from Sir Alfred for seed money to jump-start her company. VeganVegas Lotions are now sold around the world, and she has distribution plants in each major country.

Kitty and Prince Cloverdale are an item and her ideas with leprechaun branding has, well, I know you've seen the product placements in the television shows and movies.

Sir Alfred and Mildred moved into a house in the neighborhood of Las Vegas where they would host whoever happens to be in residency.

Ben and Finn are a couple, and Mildred came to realize Ben had other reasons for canoodling with Finn, and she was okay with her son's lifestyle.

Elmville and Drurie are trademarked and in case you're wondering, Elmville never did apologize for framing Drurie with the potato famine debacle. Brothers! Am I right!!

And if you're asking about the locked door at Castle Whitestone, well, the leprechauns have to keep some secrets.

Chas, well, Chas was flipping the sign on the street corner, advertising the free breakfast buffet at one of the second seed casinos.

Which proves to one and all.
Never make fun of superstitions
AND…
Never talk when you should be listening.

A word about the author…

Born with a passion to read, write and heavily influenced by Nancy Drew mysteries, Jane Greenhill recalls her first writing experiences on an old Underwood typewriter, plunking away at the keys while she wrote about hiding clues in oak trees. Fast forward through marriage and motherhood. Jane has now advanced to a laptop and her characters speak to her from other countries, planets and realms.